AZHER JIRJEES

AT REST IN THE CHERRY ORCHARD

AZHER JIRJEES

AT REST IN THE CHERRY ORCHARD

Translated from the Arabic by Jonathan Wright

At Rest in the Cherry Orchard
First published in English translation
by Banipal Books, London, 2024

Arabic copyright © Azher Jirjees
English translation copyright © Jonathan Wright, 2024
al-Nawm fi Haql al-Karaz was first published in Arabic in 2019
Original title: النوم في حقل الكرز
Published by Dar Al-Rafidain, Beirut, Lebanon

The moral right of Azher Jirjees to be identified as the author of
this work and of Jonathan Wright as the translator of this work
has been asserted in accordance with the Copyright, Designs and
Patents Act, 1988.

No part of this book may be reproduced in any form or by any
means without the prior written permission of the publisher

A CIP record for this book is available in the British Library
ISBN 978-1-913043-39-1
E-book: ISBN: 978-1-913043-40-7

Front cover painting: Hanoos Hanoos

Published with support from Abu Dhabi Arabic Language Center
through the Spotlight on Rights,
Abu Dhabi International Book Fair 2022

Banipal Books
1 Gough Square, LONDON EC4A 3DE, UK
www.banipal.co.uk/banipalbooks/

Banipal Books is an imprint of Banipal Publishing
Typeset in Cardo

Printed and bound in Great Britain by Clays Ltd, Elcograf S.p.A.

"Life is a cherry, death is the stone, and love is a cherry tree."
Jacques Prévert

Introduction

If the postman hadn't made a mistake, none of this would have happened. It was bitterly cold outside at the time and a heavy snowfall was blanketing the roads and the pavements. Snowflakes also covered the mailboxes and hid the names written on them. As usual, I put on a long woollen coat and a hat with two furry ear flaps. Then I pulled on my fur-lined boots and went out to check the mail. I put my hand in the mailbox and found a newspaper with an invitation card tucked between the pages. This was puzzling since I didn't have a subscription to any newspapers. I'd stopped my subscriptions when the translation agency where I work started providing the morning papers for free on the tables in the cafeteria. So where did the invitation come from, I wondered, as I turned it over.

The invitation was from the mass-circulation newspaper *Dagposten* and it wasn't addressed to anyone in particular. It was for a party to celebrate the newspaper's golden jubilee. I suspected it was meant for my neighbour, retired doctor Morten Solheim, since he was a long-standing subscriber to the newspaper. I knocked on his door but there was no answer. I phoned him in case he had had some mishap since he wasn't in the habit of sleeping so late. A voicemail message told me he had gone to Antalya in Turkey and wouldn't be back for three months. He does that every winter – travels to sunny climes in search of warmth.

I contacted the newspaper that had sent the invitation and confirmed that my theory was correct: the invitation was indeed intended for my neighbour, and it had come to me only because of the postman's error. Very graciously, the editor apologised on the postman's behalf and suggested compensating me with a slice of cake if I accepted the invitation and attended the reception. I accepted willingly of course – who turns down an invitation from a gracious woman? And the following night I was there, dressed to the nines.

It was a lavish event attended by dozens of journalists, writers, newspaper staff and readers. At the door stood an attractive woman in her forties in a long dress, wearing some heady perfume. She introduced herself as the editor in chief, Helena Jorstad. I returned her greeting and reminded her of her promise, and she laughed. After the speeches and the formal parts of the party, we met again at the buffet. She was carrying two plates, each with a piece of cake covered in chocolate. I took one and thanked her, and then we started chatting. I told her I'd liked this kind of cake since I was in Iraq, where my mother used to make it for holidays and parties. Helena stopped eating the cake as soon as she heard that. Her eyes opened wide and she rubbed her cheek with the tip of her finger. "In Iraq?" she asked. "That means you must know Said Jensen, the

Norwegian writer of Iraqi origin!" "How could I not know him?" I replied. "I regularly read the things he's had published in your paper and I've translated some of his short stories for the Arabic magazine *al-Shiraa*." Then I started listing the stories, expounding on Jensen and the bitter irony in his work. I told her about the story of the bird that lost its voice, the first one of his I had translated, and *The Sheep's Lord*, *Three on the Road* and other stories here and there. Helena listened with great interest as she tried to polish off the cake on her plate. After that she told me there was something I had to see immediately.

She invited me to her office on the second floor of the newspaper building, and I followed without asking any questions. We went into the office and she took a brown envelope out of a drawer and put it on the table. She said it contained a hand-written manuscript in Norwegian and she had been planning to publish it, but was waiting till she could find someone to translate it into Arabic.

She pulled it out of the envelope and waved it in the air. "This story by Said Jensen should first be read by those who speak his language, because of what it contains." Then she handed it to me and suggested I translate it into Arabic. I took the manuscript from her and immediately began to read the first page. Two years later, and all because of that postman's mistake, the translation is complete, and this is the story.

The translator
Oslo 2010

I know I should die where I was born
But, before that, let me finish off being born.
Sargon Boulus

1

He was standing on one leg like a statue hit by a stray piece of shrapnel. His face wasn't wholly visible because the straw hat he was wearing shaded his eyes, and his chin was covered by a white piece of cloth that had faint traces of blood on it. He was tall and thin, with a long nose that almost reached his mouth and a ragged beard that hung down from under the piece of cloth. I tried to approach him but he waved me away with his myrtle walking stick. We stood facing each other on an abandoned railway line with weeds growing up between the rusty tracks. Thick clouds were closing in, blocking out the sky and creating a dreary, stifling grey umbrella above us. The wind carried the sound of a crow cawing and of trees rustling, though none were visible around us. There was just that forgotten railway track and armies of ants carrying their winter supplies and disappearing into deep black holes in the ground. Finally he cleared his throat and, in a voice tinged with sorrow, said, "Where's my grave?" I went up to him to get a look at his face but he backed away, leaving a pool of blood behind him. A large hole stretched from under his neck to his navel. His torn, tattered and bloodied clothes showed serious damage in the lower part of his body. His only leg was connected directly to his stomach rather than to a pelvis, like a tower that has been blown over in a storm and then reassembled by a drunken monkey, or like a wall that has been destroyed by a random shell and rebuilt by an elderly cripple. I felt dizzy and collapsed to the ground. I tried to stand up again but I couldn't, while my father stepped back and moved away, after giving up hope of hearing an answer. I stretched my arm out towards him, as if begging him to take me with him, but he dissolved into smoke in the distance. Then a crow came up, flapping its wings and grabbing the myrtle stick in its beak. It threw the stick towards me and then was gone too. I took hold of the stick, leant on it and stood up. It was strong enough to help me up. I set off in the direction my father had taken along the railway track. I wanted to catch up with him and take the piece of cloth off his face, but an express train came from behind and flattened me.

I came to my senses. The coffee had boiled over so I turned off the stove. I poured what was left of it down the sink and starting making another cup. It wasn't the first time I had seen my father: he would visit from time to time, appear in front of me when my mind wandered. But despite his repeated visits, he would never show his face. His features always seemed to have disappeared and his appearance was incomplete. He visited me once on the balcony of the flat: his head had been cut off and his voice was coming out of a black hole in his neck. When

I went up to him, he disappeared into thin air. Later he appeared in front of me at the metro station, split into two halves that looked quite different. One evening I saw him sleeping near me like a piece of human dough without any covering of skin. I often saw my father, without really seeing him. I often begged him to show me his face but he would never do so.

In fact, I wouldn't know what my father looked like anyway. I've never seen him in my life and I don't have a single photograph of him. He disappeared into the realms of oblivion before I came into the world and, on the day he was arrested, my mother burned all his books, papers, diaries and photo albums. That's what she told me. One night, in a low voice, she told me that in a moment of fear and panic she opened the clay oven and threw in everything that belonged to my father or that hinted at his existence, and everything that made her anxious for his sake. My mother fed the memories of a whole life to the oven, and the damned fire turned them into worthless ashes, the last trace of my father disappearing along with any future he might have had. He was a leftist opponent of the government and a wanted man. He had been imprisoned several times, and then released. Every time he came out he was missing another tooth, which meant that despite his young age, he had dentures on both his upper and lower jaws. But the last time he didn't come home. They said he had died under torture, they said he had been fed alive to dogs, they said he had been thrown into the tight-lipped River

Tigris, and they said he had been secretly buried in some graveyard. But they never gave us a body or any bones, or even a certificate to say he had departed this world. When I was five years old, my mother told me: "Your father's in good hands." And when I asked her whose good hands he was in, she scolded me without explanation.

I went to bed after two thirds of the night had already passed. I turned out the light and put the sheet over my face in the hope of stealing a short nap, but it was no use. I couldn't get the image of my father with his broken body out of my mind and that made it impossible to sleep. I threw off the cover and went to the study. I was met by the empty frame hanging on the wall. I felt it was slightly tilted, so I put my index finger under the right-hand corner and pushed it up gently until it was level. Then I sat at the computer trying to get my father's ghost out of my head. I browsed the byways of the Internet far and wide. In the end I came across a poem by Badr Shakir al-Sayyab on a literary forum: "They stick out their necks from the thousands of graves, shouting at me / To come – a blood-curdling, bone-shaking call that scatters ashes on my heart. / The late afternoon here is like a torch in the shadows / Come and burn in it till sunset / My grandfathers and forefathers are a mirage that hovered on my cheek." I let out a sigh, and al-Sayyab moved on, thundering in his sad voice: "My mother calls from the grave, 'Embrace me, my son, for I have the coldness of ruination in my veins;

warm my bones with the clothes on your arms and chest, and dress the wounds.'"

"My God! How come I can't escape the sound of graves tonight?" I said to myself. I was about to turn off the computer, but then I remembered that I hadn't opened my email since the previous Saturday. It had been such an exhausting week that I hadn't had a chance to sit down and look through my messages. I opened my inbox and found some emails that were not very important. They were warnings to pay late bills, an invitation to take part in a workers' protest to demand a small salary increase, and advertisements from new companies. But finally I found an unexpected message from Baghdad, dated the previous Saturday. It read:

"Hi Said. There's something important that can't be postponed.

You must come back to Baghdad immediately.

All the best,

Abir."

2

For fourteen years I've been forgotten, living here in exile like a bear that's lost his partner. In this country the winter is long and dark and the snowfalls are heavy, while the summer is shorter than a break for tea on a journey. After the alarm clock rang, and before going into the bathroom, I was in the habit of opening the window to see how much snow had fallen overnight. Every time I would see the same scene: a white cloak covering the surface of the city and workers leaving the warmth of their beds, weighed down by thick coats and furry hats. I would dismiss it grumpily with a wave of my hand and close the window. My work in the postal service was especially arduous because I had to sort hundreds of letters and parcels in the snow in the cold dawn hours. I learned that, to be a postman in a country such as Norway, you have to get used to angry skies and the taste of hell, especially in winter, what with the cold, the ice and the constant danger of slipping. But in my case it wasn't just the sky that was angry with me: my boss was too. Kari Solberg, a thin woman in her sixties with a wrinkled, ruddy face, hated me instinctively. When she saw me, it was as if a scorpion had stung her between her thighs. She couldn't bear the sound of my voice and she looked away whenever I spoke to her, as if I were a toad covered in disgusting warts. If I said, "Please look at me, Mrs Solberg," she didn't respond. She pretended not to have heard, even when we were talking about work. When I got an address wrong, she used vitriolic, disgusting, hair-raising language.

Once, speaking to my colleague Daniel, she said, "Listen, Daniel, I can't bear that monkey Said. You should keep away from him as much as you can during work hours." I'm much more handsome than a monkey, of course, but whenever I see her angry, there's a question that nags at me: why does this woman hate monkeys so much? Why can't she bear to look at their cute faces? I, for example, have never done anything to anger her, although I would like to do so, and I've never been negligent in my work with her. So what, I wonder, lies behind all this hatred? At first I thought there must be some grudge she wanted to pursue against me, but over time I discovered that she didn't like foreigners in general and couldn't bear to look at them. In fact, I was certain she considered them all to be monkeys, even if they happened to have blue eyes. I was also certain that, however hard I worked, I would remain suspect in her eyes, and in the end this forced me into social isolation. At seven in the morning I would arrive to pick up the mail, put it in the van and go around delivering until four in the afternoon, without speaking to anyone or even meeting anyone. In this way Kari Solberg made me feel as lonely as a leper.

3

The darkness finally dissipated and dawn started to etch its lines on the face of creation. I hadn't slept a single hour. Anxieties were burrowing away in my skull, like termites in wood. I tossed and turned in bed as I pondered Abir's last message: "You must come back to Baghdad immediately." What could I do there? She must have been joking. I had written to her, asking for an explanation, but she hadn't replied. Her internet access was through local top-up cards and it ran at the speed of an overweight tortoise. I went to the kitchen, drank a glass of water and went back to bed.

In all the time I had known her, Abir had never written such an obscure message. I came across her by accident when I was sitting at the computer one day, reading the news on a website. I caught sight of an interesting article on cemeteries in Iraq. That was exactly two years ago. When I read the article, I imagined my father's body lying on its back in a hole lit by the moon. I called out to him but a cloud of black bats blocked out the light and he disappeared. I looked up the name of the journalist who had written the article and ended up on her personal website. With one click, her personal details leapt up in front of me like salmon in a river: Abir Kazim, journalist and photographer, born in Baghdad, BA in journalism, participant in several local and international projects, works as a news correspondent for the BBC. "Great!" I shouted, clicked on the link to photographs of her, and gasped like a teenager when a beautiful woman walks past. She won my heart from the first gasp and held her place there, unchallenged – a woman of medium height, as slim as an orchid and meek as a dove. Abir had eyes the colour of honey and short hair the colour of dates. In the middle of her left cheek she had a beauty spot that a bird might mistake for a mustard seed. In all the photos she was wearing a blouse and grey skirt that ended a fraction of an inch above the knee. She looked like a well-dressed student in university attire. I copied her email address and sent her an instant message: "Good evening. I'm Said, an Iraqi in the land of ice. If you wish, I can most solemnly swear that if you reply to this message, I will not only be happy, as my name Said implies, but Asaad, very happy indeed." Her answer came the next day: "Welcome, Asaad," it said. Since then we have been exchanging emails and transcontinental e-kisses.

4

I silenced the alarm clock when it screeched at me at six in the morning. I should have turned it off the night before, because I didn't need it. My long vacation had started and I wouldn't have to see Kari Solberg's face for three whole weeks. I tried to get back to sleep, but it was no use: some messages keep you awake and shatter the peace of mind that protects you. Why did Abir want me to come back immediately, I wondered. Why now in particular? Going back to Baghdad became fashionable back in April 2003. At the time, thousands of Iraqis left their places of exile and returned voluntarily, some of them hungry for power like hungry dogs, some of them to invest their assets in projects they thought would yield pure gold without taxes, and others in the belief that Iraq was now open-minded enough to tolerate them. I had seen them packing their bags, putting arduous years of exile behind them, but I never thought of doing likewise. I never said to myself, even hypothetically, "Why not go back home?" For me the answer to the question was a foregone conclusion.

I'm well aware that Abir loves Baghdad, even in its recent state of ruin, and she isn't thinking of leaving, but we have never spoken about the question of returning before. Over two years she has never once asked me about it. What's happened now, for God's sake? I pushed the bed cover off and went to the bathroom. It was raining heavily outside, although it was summer. I took the electric razor out of the drawer and started trimming my beard. It was long and shaggy and ugly. Unusually for me, I had a close look at myself in the mirror, and saw that a grey horde had made inroads from my scalp. My sideburns were tinged with grey and there were plenty of white hairs at the roots near my parting. Why hadn't I seen them before? Or rather, why was it today in particular that I was interested in counting the white hairs on my head? Did Abir's message have anything to do with it? I don't know.

I finished shaving and showering and went off to the kitchen naked. Being naked is the only good thing about living alone. Being alone means you can take your clothes off whenever you want and let the air brush your skin. I washed the dishes that had been gathering in the sink for days, then took some bread out of the freezer and put it in the oven. I rinsed out the teapot, filled it with water and put it on the stove. I threw in two cardamom pods and waited till it started to boil. Then I put in three teaspoonfuls of the Sri Lankan tea sold by Kaka Sirvan, the Kurdish owner of the oriental grocery in the neighbourhood. I took the tea off the stove, left it to brew in peace, and went back to the bedroom. I got dressed and splashed a little aftershave behind my ears. I put the bottle back in its place and looked in the mirror. The black rings under my eyes were growing larger and the grey hairs made me uneasy. I opened the drawer and took out a small pair of scissors. I cut off a thin streak of grey that was hanging over my forehead, and another one that was buried in my moustache. I cut off three hairs that were hiding in my sideburns, then moved the scissors closer to my parting to stop the damned greyness sneaking out of the follicles. But I felt it was futile, because such a small pair of scissors couldn't erase the effects of time and exile on my face. "It's quite clear. You've grown old, Said," the mirror said. "A day in exile has the same aging effect as three normal days." I didn't care. I abandoned it to its nonsense and left the room.

The smell of bread from the kitchen filled the sitting room. The tea was ready too. I took two eggs out of the fridge, boiled them and cut them into round slices. Next to them I put a piece of salty cheese and five olives. I didn't put five intentionally, of course, they were what was left in the jar. I finished breakfast before seven o'clock and sat in front of the television in all my elegance. I picked up the remote and started switching between channels. I hadn't been inclined to sit rooted in front of the television before, but I'd become addicted as soon as the drums of war started beating two years earlier, when the word Baghdad was always in the headlines. At the time, the world was interested in us and I had spent the whole night switching channels and following the breaking news that appeared at the bottom of the screen. Sitting on the same sofa in the sitting room, I had watched the UN inspectors leaving Baghdad and listened to the speech in which the US president gave his Iraqi counterpart forty-eight hours to leave the country or face war. After the deadline passed, I read on the same screen the urgent news that zero hour had come and that the allies had launched missiles against strategic targets in Baghdad. My friend Jamal Saadoun called me that day to tell me the good news, as if they were announcing the sighting of the new moon and the start of the feast after Ramadan. He was overjoyed to see the night sky over Baghdad lit up like day as multiple smart bombs exploded. "Have you seen what's happening, Said?" he said. "Didn't I tell you this day was bound to come? It's all over, all over. Hurrah, hurray."

"What's all over, Jamal? And what's to celebrate? The country's on fire, man, and people are dying."

"No one will die, believe me. They know what they're doing. We'll finally get rid of the tyrant, and Iraq will become a paradise like Las Vegas."

I don't know who had told him that. He swore that serious multinational corporations were waiting on the borders for the signal to go in, and they would transform the country.

"You're right, we'll get rid of the tyrant. But Iraq becoming a paradise like Las Vegas? Is that the joke of the season?" I had commented, once my friend was done with his torrent of solemn oaths to the truth of what he'd said. He didn't like what I said and hung up without saying goodbye. Then I suddenly had a terrible headache, concentrated as usual in the back of my head, and it forced me to visit the doctor.

5

The city was decorated for Christmas and snowflakes were falling slowly, combining with the lights to create an otherworldly ambiance I had never seen before. I stood at the bus stop in my long woollen coat, planning to go to the library. I wanted to borrow a book about photography, a medium that I love, although I rarely use my camera and I'm lazy about changing the batteries, which went flat long ago. The bus finally arrived. I greeted the driver, then reached into my coat pocket for some money for the bus fare. But I couldn't find my wallet. I remembered that I'd left it on the bedside table. I slapped myself on the forehead and shouted: "*Khara bil-kaa'inat!*" The driver laughed at me swearing in Arabic and said, "Never mind, get on." He paid the fare from his own pocket and gave me a ticket. He was a young man with a distinctly Arab face, in his thirties, of medium height, with dark, deep-set eyes in a thin face and a small, trimmed beard. I thanked him and sat down in the seat immediately behind him. He laughed away as he repeated the expletive I had used. "You reminded me of what our people say, man," he explained. Now I knew he was Iraqi, though at first I had thought him Palestinian. Then we started chatting and exchanged telephone numbers. Jamal Saadoun, the immigrant bus driver, thus became the only Iraqi in Scandinavia who knew my telephone number.

Since I had met him, Jamal had been tirelessly counting the days till the fall of the regime and a change of government in Iraq. He never harboured any doubts, never gave up hope that the moment would come. When it did come, as one of the countless victims of that repressive regime, he danced for joy till dawn. He had graduated from the engineering faculty at Mustansiriyah University and worked as an engineer for the Baghdad municipality. Once he had settled into his job, he asked to marry the neighbours' daughter and was about to move on from bachelorhood. But because he had a beard and frequented mosques, informers, who were thick on the ground at the time, decided to keep a close eye on him and provide their masters with secret reports full of fabricated intrigues. In the end he was arrested on a charge of treason and news of him was as hard to find as the remains of a cat that strays into a cave full of starving dogs.

6

The librarian pointed to a rectangular brass plaque that said Photography in black enamel. It was on a large shelf of books and rare magazines on photography. I went over, picked out one of the books and sat down at a table to have a quick browse. On page 27 I saw a black-and-white photograph of a glider that took part in the Vietnam war, according to the caption below. The commander of the glider was giving a V-for-victory sign after unloading a pile of bombs onto the heads of the inhabitants. I remembered the sound of the first warplane I ever heard. I was nine years old at the time, playing ball in the alleyway with my friends when an air raid siren sounded and we ran home in panic. I went and hid under my mother's long dress, and awaited disaster. Some warplanes flew over at low altitude and the sound was deafening. My mother put her hands over my ears and recited from the Qur'an: "*Bardan wa salaaman. Bardan wa salaaman.* Cool and safe. Cool and safe", until the sound of the planes receded into the distance. I looked into my mother's eyes and saw a fear that would last a long time. In the meantime someone pulled out a chair and sat at the table. I came to my senses: I had my hands clasped around my head and I was chanting "*Bardan wa salaaman*" repeatedly.

7

Treason is well-known as an accusation made by bastards more often than drunks sing *Atlal*, that song by Umm Kulthoum. "You're a traitor" is an easy, readily made charge, like pot noodles. But these characteristically Arab noodles can easily lead you to the gallows and bring shame on those you leave alive behind you. Oddly, this vile charge is often thrown in your face without explanation or justification. You may not know what form your treason took or when or where or on whose behalf you committed the crime. Someone has simply called you a traitor and that is the end of the matter. There is nothing you can do then other than admit total surrender, sign a confession to treason, and then prepare to walk fearlessly to the gallows and put up with eternal shame.

The news that Jamal Saadoun was a traitor didn't reach his family: he languished in the dungeons of the feared military intelligence department for two whole years. He saw the sun only twice during that period, firstly for the annual delousing session and secondly when he had a burst appendix and was taken to hospital to have it removed. He was lucky nonetheless: he was released under a general amnesty decreed by the president and went back to his family. He says that when he came out of prison his father, al-Hajj Saadoun, who was waiting for him at the main gate, didn't recognise him. Because of hunger, fear and maltreatment, Jamal had lost two thirds of his weight and was as pale as a lemon. He was shocked by the looks of uncertainty in his father's eyes. He went right up to him and said, "Don't you recognise me, Dad? I'm Jamal." His father fainted in shock and the agal around his keffiyeh fell off. His mother, who was standing behind the door at home, watching the street, bewailed the state of the remaining third of her returning son. The woman wept and screamed, beat her chest and rolled on the floor when she saw him coming towards her like a ghost from the vaults of hunger. Every time she beat her chest or forehead, fearlessly and without inhibition she cursed those who had done this to her son. In the end his father had to silence her by force for fear the security men might come back and arrest Jamal again. "Enough shouting and cursing, woman," he said. "The walls have ears."

The times indeed dictated that such curses could only be whispered and were best left unspoken. The walls did have ears, as many fathers believed. But the returning son didn't tell his parents the whole story. If he had told them, the screaming would have brought the roof down. He told me the most horrific part of it, however.

He said the interrogating officer amused himself by stripping him naked and attached an electric wire to his penis. This had made him permanently impotent, he said.

"That's impossible! You must be joking," I said.

"Really, Said? Would I joke about such a thing?"

It wasn't a joke, as I had stupidly thought. Who would joke about his manhood? Jamal realised he had become sexually impotent when he was in jail. The interrogator had routinely attached the wire to his penis, saying, "You won't get out of here until I've killed it for you", and the bastard had carried out his threat. The tons of Viagra that Jamal consumed after coming out of jail had not given him a single moment of sexual pleasure with a woman.

8

On April 9, 2003, an American tank recovery vehicle drove into Firdos Square, surrounded by dozens of civilians, and brought down the statue of the dictator – a symbol that Baghdad had fallen and that the city and Iraq as a whole were completely under control. Soon after that the satellite channels started carrying pictures of people looting and starting fires. Bands of thugs, thieves and Baathist goons attacked government offices to loot them and destroy what was left of them, as tough US marines looked on. They seemed to be working together to destroy the country, not just the regime. Jamal Saadoun phoned me at the time and told me he had decided to go back to Baghdad and wouldn't wait another day. He was going to help rebuild the country, to use his expression. In order to preserve our good friendship, I didn't object to his decision or make any direct comment, but I joked with him, since a joke is a safe way to convey an idea without doing any harm. "Okay, boss," I said, "so you've decided to go to Las Vegas!"

"Is Your Highness making fun of me?" he replied, with an affected chuckle that didn't disguise his irritation.

"Don't get upset, I'm just kidding. Anyway, please be careful and give my regards to Baghdad," I said in farewell.

"Okay, I will. So long," he said, and then hung up.

9

The only relatives I had left in Baghdad were my mother and my uncle Ibrahim, whom I couldn't stand. He was a vacuous Baathist with a bushy moustache. He wore an olive-green suit and from his belt hung a 9 mm pistol engraved with a portrait of Tariq ibn Ziyad, the commander of the Muslim army that invaded Spain. Like other Baathists at the time, he had a large belly that hung out in front like a balloon full of water, and he carried under his arm a newspaper that he didn't usually read.

"Papa Aflaq has arrived, get ready for the bullshit," I would say, to tease my mother whenever Uncle Ibrahim was coming to visit us, and she would laugh. I nicknamed him Papa Aflaq because he was obsessed with collecting pamphlets written by Michel Aflaq, one of the founders of the Baath Party, though he never read a single line in any of them. He was obsessed with these pamphlets in the same way as he was obsessed with hanging up pictures of the president and carrying the loathsome party newspapers under his arm. I couldn't stand this arrogant, odious man who ate with his mouth open. If it hadn't been for his son Jalal, who was about my age and loved my mother as much as I did, I would never have stepped foot in their house. One day Jalal invited me to lunch. Uncle Ibrahim had hung up a giant picture of the president across the wall in the guest room. I remember it was a colour photograph in a gilt wooden frame and it showed the dictator standing and praying close to the lattice screen around the tomb of some holy man.

"There is no power or strength other than in God. That man's so pious he's going to weep," I joked when I saw it.

"Please, Said, I beg you," Jalal replied. "Stop making sarcastic comments in case my father hears you."

But his father had heard me, I don't know how, and he started telling me off. We got into an argument and I left their house before lunch was served. He was rude and disrespectful to those around him, and for years he broke my mother's heart by describing my father and his political colleagues as traitors. In fact, the only sin my mother ever committed was deciding to be a mother in Iraq. She had bad luck and her few moments of happiness would amount to a story of very few pages. That story of happiness would begin when my father chose her as his partner in life; it ended three months after they were married. One night heavily armed men broke into the house, beat him up in front of her and dragged him off to a vehicle, whereupon he disappeared, leaving a wound in her heart that never healed. He loved her, my mother says, despite the short time they lived together under the same roof, and he was at a loss as to how he might make her happy. Despite his ideological position, he respected what she believed in and prayed to. Once she told me he loved *maqam* music and especially the singer Nazim al-Ghazali. He would sit in the courtyard of the house in the evening to smoke cigarettes and sway to the poems al-Ghazali sang:

A dove came and cooed beside me,
Neighbour, I said, do you know the state I'm in?
Love forbid, you've never tasted the pain of parting,
And nothing has ever troubled your mind.
Can feathers carry someone whose heart is saddened
To a high branch in the far distance?
Neighbour, fate has not been fair to either of us,
Come and we can share worries with each other, come.

But when he saw her slip into the room to pray, he stopped playing the record until she had finished. Nothing is better than love at making different beliefs acceptable. My mother burned even those Ghazali records when she set about destroying almost everything that might remind her of my father. All that remained of him was an Indian-made bicycle and an Orient wristwatch. In the end, my mother had to sell them, along with some of the furniture, to buy a Singer sewing machine, which was a feature in almost every Iraqi house at the time. I would see her sitting at the Singer tirelessly, night and day, in order to provide for me. She was in the same position as hundreds of other widows whose husbands had been swallowed up by the prisons and who remained loyal to their memory. Umm Said, my mother, showed the door to all those who came seeking her hand. She took up sewing so that she could feed me without us having to humiliate ourselves. Our life was bitter in Baghdad. No one there offered us any help, not even Uncle Ibrahim, who treated us as if we carried a disease and he was worried we might infect him. My mother would constantly remind me of her relationship with her husband, my father Nassir Mardan, the teacher who lost his life because he wasn't content just to dream of freedom, but went further and spoke out about his dream. She wanted to fix the story in my memory and impress on my mind's eye an image of him being dragged off to his demise, so that I would learn by heart the principle that speaking about freedom under a repressive regime was like having sex in the street in the middle of the day. "Be careful, Said. The walls have ears," she would say over and over until I had learned the lesson well, writing it out in my notebooks, on my wrist and on my pillow. On the wall I drew big ears to save her the bother of repeating her words of warning. I did all this to put my mother's heart at ease and reassure her that the tragedy would not recur. But I never did promise to stop making fun of Papa Aflaq and his big belly.

10

Around noon one scorching day Papa Aflaq came around, frothing at the mouth. With his usual arrogance, he said that the children of traitors couldn't obtain certificates of "ideological probity" and so I wouldn't get a place in university, at least until cocks laid eggs. Before I could answer, he shouted in my face that he wasn't planning to have a quiet word with any of his colleagues in the party to help me obtain such a certificate. I was about to crown him with the mug I was holding but my mother came between us and pushed me away. Then he stormed out, making threats and hurling insults about my father and mother. At the front door, my mother just said to him, "There is a god" and turned back, keeping her sadness to herself.

That year I had passed my baccalaureate exams and had applied for a place in the Humanities Faculty of Baghdad University. But the "ideological probity" requirement seemed likely to dash my dreams of studying literature. The regime set obstructive conditions for applicants for university places, the most important of which were "ideological probity" and "loyalty to the Revolution". I was on tenterhooks waiting for fate to hear my mother's prayers and do away with this requirement. In the end, after my mother had prostrated herself in prayer for me seven thousand times in the dead of night, someone knocked on the door. It was the *mukhtar*, a local dignitary by the name of Abu Shaalan, who looked like fate's merciful messenger. He told me the selection process was done and dusted. "And how did it go?" I asked impatiently. He said he had received a request for information about me from the local branch of the party. He told them I was "ideologically sound" and not hostile to either the party or the Revolution, and so my application was accepted. What a pitiful system that was, where Abu Shaalan the *mukhtar* was the judge of sound and unsound ideology! And what a pitiful life we led under the protection of Papa Aflaq and his colleagues!

Anyway, confirmation that I had a place in the Humanities Faculty arrived and I joined the Arabic language department. It was the only time I tasted happiness. As I went through the various stages of my course at university with success, I felt my dream had come true and I was making good progress on my journey into the world of writing. But fate changed its mind just before I reached the finishing line. One day I was on my way to the library to borrow some reference books for my graduation dissertation when one of my colleagues called me. "Said, Said, please wait," he said. He was a busybody who liked to stick his nose in other people's business, and no one could stand him. He had transferred from another university at the beginning of that year. I remember he had borrowed my copies of the "national culture" lectures, part of a dreadful course the Ministry of Higher Education had inserted into the syllabus to pollute our minds with nonsense about the Baath Party and the Revolution. I stopped, turned to him and said, "Yes, buddy, what's up?" He gave the lectures back to me with a smile.

"Thanks. The comments in the footnotes made me laugh!" he said.

"What comments?"

"The ones written in ink at the bottom."

He was referring to random comments I had written to relieve the tedium of reading the text. "That's because the national culture course is worse than an unwanted guest on your wedding night," I joked, and we laughed.

I borrowed the complete works of al-Mutanabbi and Ibn al-Anbari's commentary on the Muallaqat poems from the library. On the way the busybody said the next lecture would be in two hours and he invited me to a cup of tea in the cafeteria. I accepted his invitation and we turned towards the students' club, where we had tea and chatted. I discovered he was a nice person and I regretted having thought of him as a busybody. We chatted about the university, our graduation dissertations and the approaching exams, and then we reverted to the ridiculous "national culture" professor, who was rather like Uncle Ibrahim when it came to his paunch, his moustache and his intellectual inadequacy. I made much fun of the man, thanked my host for the tea and went to the photocopying office to copy some papers. After that we often met outside the lecture hall and the barriers between us started to fall like dominoes. In the end he managed to win my trust, and we became inseparable. I liked his wit: he always remembered the latest jokes current in Iraq and the wider Arab world. Once while we were sitting in the students' club, he mimicked the dictator in a joke and we laughed quietly for fear of informers. "You're quite a joker!" I told him as I laughed.

"Okay," he replied, with his usual spontaneity, "you tell us one, and make sure it's funnier than the national culture lectures."

"Okay, I said, "listen to this one. The president visited a chicken farm one day and told the chickens they had to lay five eggs every day and if any of them failed to meet the target he would have their heads cut off and have them thrown to the dogs. The chickens were terrified and they all laid exactly five eggs each. The president went around picking up the chickens one by one. When he found five eggs, he nodded and said 'Well done', his favourite expression. But finally he picked up a chicken and found only one egg. He knitted his bushy eyebrows and shouted, 'Didn't I say five eggs?' 'B-b-but Mister P-p-president, I'm a cock.'"

My friend chuckled away. "Even chickens aren't safe from him," he said, and we parted.

11

In the distance I could see my mother standing at the bus stop. She was wearing an abaya and watching the road. She had sneaked over the roof into the home of our neighbour, Hajj Zaini, and then out of their back door to the street. Then she walked towards the main street till she reached the bus stop. When she saw me, she grabbed my hand and pulled me aside. Breathlessly, she told me they were looking for me and she had chosen this secret route for fear they might follow me and grab me, and that I had to hide immediately. I didn't understand a thing she said. She was gripped with fear like an animal pursued by a marauding tiger. She was so frightened she couldn't even complete her sentences properly. All I could hear was the sound of her heart beating. I urged her to calm down and explain what was going on. Who are these people who were looking for me? Why should I hide when I hadn't done anything to justify such alarm? She pretended to calm down, but to no avail. Her heart was still beating like a drum and her lips were trembling like a butterfly's wings. In the end I gathered that a posse of security men had raided the house looking for me and they still hadn't left the lane.

That busybody had recorded my voice on a device hidden in his jacket pocket and handed it to the security people, so now I was a wanted man because of a silly joke. I suggested my mother go home discreetly, and I fled immediately to Uncle Ibrahim's house. As soon as I got there, I told Jalal what had happened and asked him to keep it a secret, for fear that Papa Aflaq might find out and hand me over to the police in chains.

Midnight came and I slipped back home. I found Mother crying at the door, afraid and uncertain what the future held for me. Almost in a whisper, she said they would come back for me and wouldn't give up. She had a mother's certainty that the noose would tighten and I was bound to fall into their hands, like a mouse in a trap. At the time I wasn't as worried about what had happened, or would happen, as I was about the state my mother was in. What an ordeal the heavens had inflicted on her! What bad luck she had, being a mother in Iraq! To be a mother in Iraq was an inauspicious fate. The country would never tire of tormenting mothers.

She took me in, bolted the door and gave me a bundle of dinars tied together with some woollen yarn. "You can't live here any longer," she said. "Take this money and leave the country before I lose you and you break my heart."

"Where did you get this from?"

"I sold the sewing machine this morning. I don't need it. Leave, I beg you."

"Where should I go, Mama?" I asked.

"It's a big wide world, my son," she replied.

12

Countries grow weak when war consorts with them. Counterfeit goods proliferate and forgers emerge as rising stars. Jalal took me to Munir the Jackal, the most famous forger in Baghdad and its suburbs, who said the passports he issued were much better than the ones issued by the state and that every single forged document in the city had passed through his deft hands. He was a stocky man in his twenties with a dark face, no more than five foot three tall, with thick black hair and a large nose stuck on his face like a frog's arse. I wanted to ask why he was nicknamed the Jackal, but I thought it wiser to keep quiet in case the greedy opportunist blew a fuse and charged me double. I gave him a passport photo and the first instalment of the fee. He told me the passport would be ready within two days. When we left, I turned to Jalal and asked: "Where did you come across this scumbag?"

"One day you'll thank God for putting him in your path," he replied.

When night fell across the city, I slipped home. My mother was waiting anxiously by the door as usual. It's terrible the way mothers, devoured by dread, have to wait behind doors. Before I could say a word, she asked me what I had done, and I told her things were going well and I would soon be travelling. She burst into tears and made no comment at all. I hugged her and whispered in her ear jokingly, "Never mind, Mama, you'll get married and forget me." She smiled as she patiently wiped away her tears with her handkerchief, then held my head to her chest and started to whisper a lengthy prayer.

Two days later I picked up my bag and left home. Mother didn't say goodbye to me at the door and didn't sprinkle water on the path behind me, as Iraqi mothers would normally do in such a situation. She forced her way into the taxi, obstinately rejecting my appeals to her to stay. She sat down next to me on the back seat, while my cousin Jalal sat in the front next to the driver. She held my arm with a trembling hand, her chest heaving. She slipped an amulet on a chain around my neck, then closed her eyes and whispered Qur'anic verses and magic spells rapidly into my ear. We reached Hafiz al-Qadi Square, where the buses to Amman gathered at the time. I could see she was holding back her sobs so as not to attract the driver's attention. I squeezed her hand and planted a kiss on her head. She put her face against my neck and took a deep breath. Then she broke into tears like a cloud bursting. Her heart was beating so fast I thought it might stop. I hugged her, rubbed her shoulders and begged her to calm down, but it was no use. At the bus door Jalal tried to console her: "Don't worry about Said, Auntie, and don't be sad he's leaving. He'll be back one day, rest assured." But the way she looked at me when I waved to her through the window suggested she didn't believe I would ever come back.

13

The yelling on the talk shows was about to do my head in. I turned the television off and put the remote back on the table. My mind was still going over Abir's last message: "You must come back to Baghdad immediately." I fetched the laptop from the bedroom and put it on the dining table in the sitting room, waiting for a second message to explain what was happening. I tried to allay my anxieties by staying as calm as I could. "Why should I go back now? What's happening in Baghdad for God's sake?" I mumbled as I went into the kitchen to pamper myself with a cup of coffee. My phone rang. It was Kari Solberg calling. I ignored the call. She called again, and again I ignored it. The third time I took the call.

"Yes, Mrs Solberg, what's up?"

"There's an emergency. You have to come, Said."

"But I'm on holiday. What's happened?"

"Daniel's had an accident."

"What? Did you say Daniel's had an accident?"

"Yes, it happened just now and you'll have to come in and do his round. Take a taxi at company expense and come quickly. Please," she said.

Daniel Larsen, when I first met him in the post office, was a corpulent man in his twenties, with a head as round as a watermelon and a stomach like a sack of potatoes. He was friendly and cooperative. He could see I was lost that day sorting the letters on the afternoon shift, so he volunteered to help me. He taught me how to sort the letters and parcels by postcode and showed me the quickest ways to do the job. I stuck with him as I progressed to become a trainee postman. We went out together to deliver letters until I remembered the streets and the addresses and was assigned a van of my own. Daniel was so jovial it could be hard to tell if he was serious or joking. But despite his humour he handled Kari Solberg like a wise old man. He never objected to her endless nonsense and never complained. He said his Icelandic father had taught him how to be a sponge that soaked up other people's anger, so that life could continue without any hassle. Apart from that, he could make a silly joke out of anything, and I would laugh at him laughing and at the way his eyes sank into their sockets whenever he smiled. Once he asked me if I had ever heard of an Icelandic wizard who farted and flew at the same time. When I said "No", he said, "Neither have I", and then he roared with laughter till he had tears in his eyes.

One icy winter's day our van got stuck in the snow. We tried to get it out but we couldn't, so then we had to call the tow truck company and ask for help. The man at the company said he would send a truck but it would take about an hour to arrive because of the heavy snow. It was still early in the day and we had plenty of letters to deliver. "Why wait without working?" I said to Daniel, "What do you say we sort the letters we have left until help arrives?" He thought that was a good idea, so he took the brown sack from the back seat and we started sorting them by postcode. There were three hundred and eighty letters and sixty parcels. We started sorting them by streets, and my hand fell upon an unusual-looking parcel. It was wrapped in brown paper, came from a shop that hadn't shown its name and address, and was addressed to my unmarried neighbour, Cathrine Andersson. I examined it carefully, turned it over several times and tried to feel what it contained. My suspicions grew and the devil whispered in my ear: "Open it, Said, open it." Since I'm quick to respond to the devil in such situations, I opened the package and was surprised to find a battery-operated vibrator.

"My god! What's this, Cathrine? Why did you order this? Are men so hard to find that you have to resort to this horrible device?" I said in shock. A statuesque beauty such as Cathrine Andersson could find something much better than this, without needing to pay for packing and postage. The subject troubled me so much that I decided not to put it in her post box. It would be terrible for such a beautiful unmarried woman to use a plastic cylinder of this kind. If it was up to me, I would ban the use of such devices in even the bleakest of circumstances, because if such products were widely used, God forbid, we men would inevitably be doomed to extinction. I stuffed it into my jacket pocket and when we'd finished our round, we went to Kari Solberg's house and put it in her post box, in the hope it might distract her from harassing us. "Take that, you bitch. It's just what you need."

The next day I stayed away from work, so Daniel had to face Kari's anger alone like a proper sponge. But I made it up to him later by buying him a beer and a slice of pizza. He ate pizza insatiably and drank beer in the morning, in the evening, and any time in between. He went to bed drunk, woke up drunk and drove the post office van drunk. Once, chatting over work, I asked him if he was happy with his life.

"I don't know," he replied.

"Daniel, what do you mean you don't know?"

"I really don't know, Said, but in the end it's a short film."

"A short film?"

"Yes, life's a short film in which we all have a role to play and then we leave. Whenever disaster strikes, you just have to repeat to yourself, 'It's a short film, a short film, a short film.'"

"And why do you have to do that, you chubby philosopher?"

"So that the disaster doesn't matter so much and just

melts away like snow in the sun."

"Very well, then tell me: do you like this short film?"

"Very much."

"What exactly do you like about it?"

"Mmmm, I like three heroes in it."

"Really? And who might they be?"

"My father, pizza and that whore."

"That whore? Who might she be?"

"Beer, beer, Said. I love it like my father, and more."

Daniel called beer "the whore" because it gave pleasure in exchange for cash, as he put it. He spent two thirds of his salary on beer and the other third on food, clothes and other things. One day he drank so much he lost consciousness, and if it hadn't been for one of the people in his building he would have lost his life. That day he had drunk countless bottles of beer and poured many of them over his head and body until he fainted. The beer flooded his flat and started to seep under the door and into the corridor. It even ran down the staircase till it reached the bottom floor. One of the residents came out of his flat to throw a bag of rubbish in the bin and saw the beer trickling down the stairs and gathering in a pool near the door. The man traced the liquid back to its source: Daniel's flat on the fifth floor. He knocked on the door but no one answered, although the beer was still flowing under the door. He called the emergency services and they came and rescued Daniel.

In fact I can't confirm this story: I don't know whether it really happened or was a figment of Daniel's imagination, but that was what Daniel told me as he drove the post van drunk.

"The whore has killed you, my friend," I said to myself, as I imagined Daniel spattered with blood behind the steering wheel, like a piglet in a slaughterhouse.

"Okay, okay, I'll be there in half an hour," I told my boss and hung up. I got changed into my work jacket and called the taxi company. Exactly half an hour later I was in the post office, listening under duress to that grey-haired old lady, Kari Solberg. She seemed to be in a conciliatory mood this time, since I was on my summer leave and didn't need to help her out. I had agreed to work for the sake of my good friend Daniel. I left Solberg's office and started to unload the post bags from Daniel's van, which the road maintenance company had brought back from the scene of the accident. I put the bags on the back seat and set off to deliver them. "Why must I go back to Baghdad, I wonder?" I said to myself as I worked.

14

Midday came and there were still post bags piled up on the back seat. I had a terrible headache by this time and I was wandering around like a lost dog barking aimlessly. The headache had been troubling me for so long I suspected I had a malicious tumour somewhere in my brain. Because of it I had been to see Dr Stephan Holmberg often. This time I was complaining, to no avail, about the wooden hammers I thought were bashing my head, like the hammers in a boatyard. He would try to keep me quiet with a lousy strip of Panadol tablets, so I went back and said, "Dr Holmberg, these headaches are going to finish me off. Please put an end to them. Aren't you a doctor?" He would smile and give me the same old answer: "Don't worry, Said. It's a nervous headache that arises when you're under psychological stress. You just have to relax and it will go away."

On one occasion I told him I wouldn't leave the clinic until he put an end to it. The doctor smiled and looked down at the computer screen, searching for a suitable medicine. As he moved the mouse around, he sang a silly song: "Heaven on earth. Great joy. I'm alone. I'm alive. Heaven on earth. Great blessing. I'm alone. I'm alive."

When he was finished he swung his chair round to face me and said, "Okay, I'll give you a prescription for a recreational drug this time."

"For heaven's sake, what kind of medicine would that be?"

"Ketamine, a wonderful recreational drug. Luckily it's now available in tablet form."

I didn't know what the doctor meant by recreational drug and the fact that I didn't understand may have been obvious in my eyes, like someone who goes into a physics laboratory and doesn't even know their multiplication tables. So the man volunteered an explanation. He said it was a drug to treat psychological stress and depression and taking it in a state such as mine was sure to stop the headache in its tracks. It was also used by vets, he continued, because it calms down horses when they come around from anaesthesia in operating theatres.

"Do you think I'm a horse, to prescribe me such a drug, doctor?"

"Of course not, but a drug that can tranquillize horses, imagine how effective that would be with humans!"

"Ah, so that's it, then?"

"Yes, it is, now calm down and relax."

He took a thick book off the shelf, opened it at the index and started to run through the names of drugs till he came to ketamine. He turned to the right page and started to read the instructions to me, warning me against an overdose. He said the side effects were visual and auditory hallucinations and a sense of detachment from one's body and surroundings. As I listened to him, I felt I was on the threshold of an adventure that was likely to mess with my mind. But I accepted it because of the pain I was in, and from then on I started to take ketamine. With the passage of time, I discovered that delusions make life liveable.

Doing Daniel's shift that day, I hadn't had anything since the morning but water, tranquillizers and cigarettes. I often stopped while delivering the mail and I made many mistakes. The addresses hadn't changed and I knew them by heart. The amount of mail wasn't any different from usual, either. But when the stream of memories starts rolling, the mind gets distracted and can't concentrate. Abir had unintentionally reactivated the hard disk in my head and, as I stuffed a letter into the letter box at the main police station, I remembered how once I had stood in front of the same door in fear.

15

I was so hungry I was weak. I had forgotten to take the bag of kleicha pastries out of my suitcase before putting it in the luggage rack on the bus. The suitcase contained clothes, two packets of cigarettes and the kleicha made by my mother. She had stuffed them into the suitcase, saying, "They'll come in useful on your journey." Iraqi mothers feel at ease only when they've stuffed bags of kleicha into their sons' travel bags. After the bus had crossed the border into Jordan and was approaching the capital Amman, I asked the driver where Iraqis congregated in the city. "In the city centre, near Hashemite Square," he said.

Iraqis are rather like fish. As soon as they're out of the water, they feel they can't breathe. So when you see them anywhere abroad, you find them cutting out their own rivers and spending all their fish-lives in them. Not just that: they also have memories as short as fish. They forget traps so soon that they fall into them again. Migrant fish circled around the bus, asking for news of home, asking for cigarettes and dried food. They bought the rice, lentils and sugar that the new immigrants had filled their suitcases with, and then they left. But all I had was two packets of imported cigarettes that Jalal had given me in Baghdad, saying "Sell them when you arrive, and maybe you can raise some cash." I sold them and went off to the nearest restaurant in the city centre. It was the restaurant of a young Iraqi called Salam. I ordered a falafel sandwich with mango chutney, which was hot and delicious.

"Mmm, delicious," I said as I ordered another one.

"You're welcome. Here you are, brother," Salam replied as he handed me the second sandwich with an extra ball of falafel thrown in for free.

I felt apprehensive that day. Amman was a new city to me, with a life that was unfamiliar. New cities have frightening aspects, especially crowded ones. I didn't sit at the restaurant tables: I chewed the sandwich standing and chatted to Salam, who listened to me as he turned over the falafel in the sizzling oil. He asked when I'd arrived and why I'd come to Amman, and I summarised the story for him: "Wanderers and we ask God for help." Salam laughed and said, "We're all wanderers asking God for help." Then, by one of those rare twists of fortune, he said, "What do you say you come and work with me? I need some help." Gratefully I agreed at once, but then I remembered that I still didn't have anywhere to stay, so I added, "I just need two days to arrange somewhere to live and I'll be right back."

"Don't worry. We can arrange somewhere to stay."

"How so?"

"Come and live with me in my lodgings and we can

share the rent for the room. What do you say?"

"Of course, I agree."

"So that's that fixed then."

The next day I was standing behind the frying pan, humming along to a Fairouz song: "The wind blew on us from the valley junction / O air, let in the air and take me home."

16

Fear was my constant companion during those days. My work continued till late at night and then I had to go home alone after shutting up shop. One night two men blocked my path with a determined look in their eyes. They were policemen from the preventive security department and they asked for my papers. I handed them my passport and they said, "Come with us." They put me in the back seat of a white car, blindfolded me and drove me off into the unknown. After about a quarter of an hour, the car stopped at a metal gate. I could hear the bolt sliding open. A guard led me down a corridor that ended in a large cell full of Iraqis. "Welcome, welcome, long live Iraq the Great," one of them said. When I sat down, a friendly man in his twenties seated next to me said he had a bachelor's degree in sociology from

Baghdad University. He had come to Jordan for work and ended up as a porter in a grain warehouse until he was arrested for violating the residence regulations.

Iraqis weren't allowed to work in Jordan. They could get three-month tourist visas and after that they became easy prey for police patrols looking for immigrants. I had seen how Iraqis were abused in Jordan. They worked as porters or in construction, sold cigarettes or picked olives for low wages, and of course they didn't always get paid at all when the bosses found replacement workers and gave the old ones a casual goodbye. Often the Iraqis ended up in debt.

The next morning, they charged me with overstaying my visa and working without a permit, and I was given a choice between paying a fine of ninety Jordanian dinars, six months' imprisonment or deportation to Iraq. Because I couldn't afford to pay the fine I chose to sleep behind bars. After twenty days I was released when Salam made a bail payment, but on the way back to our lodgings he whispered in my ear that he would have to deduct the bail money from my wages, and I gratefully nodded in agreement.

Despite his gallantry, Salam was pragmatic, with little time for emotions. He kept tabs on everything in writing and treated life as a matter of addition and subtraction. He had moved to Amman after life in Iraq became unbearable and he saw no future there. One hot Iraqi day a taxi stopped outside his house with a charred corpse in a coffin, and he became the latest insignificant number on a long list of fatherless Iraqis. A soldier with one star on his epaulettes told him that his father had given his life to defend Iraqi territory and that the brigade commander and all the officers and men of the unit sent their condolences to the family. Salam's mother stood by the coffin, shrieking and banging her head against the wall until she fainted and was taken to hospital. A year after her husband's death she married his brother to save her children from a future without a father figure. But she was as unlucky as someone who finds worms in her apple: when the damned war machine stopped turning, Salam's father came back with the other prisoners-of-war. He had never died and the charred corpse they had buried years ago was someone else no one could identify. The poor man came home to find his wife in his brother's arms, properly married according to the laws of God and His prophet. Whereupon he collapsed with a heart attack and was buried in the same grave as his mysterious double. A few days later Salam's hapless mother set herself on fire and joined them, while his uncle fled to a distant town to escape the disgrace he felt through no fault of his own. This wasn't at all an Indian film: it was a quintessentially Iraqi story. In the land of fantasy, fact and fiction merge and stories are hard to believe.

Ever since I had met him, Salam made sure not a single penny slipped through his fingers. Every day, when he came home from the restaurant, he would sit down and write out his accounts in minutest detail in a big ledger that he kept under his pillow. In the expenses column he would record the cup of coffee he made for himself in the morning and drank on an empty stomach, the cigarette he smoked on his way to the restaurant, the coin he gave to a homeless man who accosted him on the way, and the piece of bread and honey he had for breakfast. At the end of the month he would tot it all up and the result would show a profit.

One long evening, I asked him whether he was tempted to stay in Amman.

"No, but thank God anyway."

"Anyway? But that means you don't feel comfortable here."

"Comfort isn't 'full-fat' unless you have nationality in the country you live in," he explained.

"Does that mean you're thinking of going back to Iraq one day?"

"What? Iraq? That's completely out of the question. I'll never forget what happened to my family there."

Salam was frightened of setting a cycle of tragedies back in motion. He saw returning to Iraq as impossible and reconciled himself to living the rest of his life in Amman.

One night I went back to our lodgings and found that a third bed had been squeezed into the room. In it was sleeping a young Iraqi who worked in the second-hand clothes trade and there were bales of old clothes stuffed under the bed. The smell would have been enough to anaesthetise a bask of crocodiles. The next day I asked

Salam about our guest and he said the owner of the building had asked if the man could stay in our room because there wasn't any other space and Salam had agreed. He said this with a wink that suggested the cost of the room would be split three ways instead of two.

Three young men who worked all day, hiding from the police patrols, and then squeezing at night into a putrid hole that wouldn't have satisfied the aspirations of a rat in the slums. It was a miserable way to live in exile from Iraq.

But it didn't last long. Early one morning the young man, who was called Mutie, went off to market with his bags and didn't come back. We went to ask after him there, and one of the traders told us the police had raided the market and taken away all the Iraqis and their goods and Mutie was among them. I felt I was now in a precarious position, like a child's baby tooth that's about to fall out, especially since the walls have ears in Amman as well as in Iraq, and someone might well give me away to the Jordanian police. Then I would inevitably be arrested and put behind bars again, or thrown over the border. My god, what should I do? Was I destined to be on the run wherever I stayed?

"A falafel sandwich, please," someone called, interrupting the anxious thoughts that troubled me.

"Coming up," I replied.

The man looked prosperous. What, I wondered, had brought him to a little falafel restaurant on the margins of life? I was about to share my thoughts with him when he graciously volunteered an explanation. As he chewed his sandwich with exaggerated relish, he said he lived in Norway in northwestern Europe and had come from the airport to the city centre in search of a falafel restaurant. He was in his late twenties, with rosy cheeks and eyes that suggested he was very happy. He had long hair and wore a gold chain and an expensive watch of the kind rich kids would have. He said he lived with his Norwegian girlfriend, they worked together in a travel and tourism company and he had come to Amman to see his mother and brothers, who would arrive from Baghdad the next day. I asked him what life was like in Norway and he said it was a paradise despite the lack of falafel, and that if my frying pan was lucky enough to get there too, then I, even me in my jeans from the second-hand clothes market, could become a wealthy businessman. I gave him another sandwich and a bottle of Mirinda on the house, and we started chatting about Norway and the kind of trousers they wore there. The man talked at length about the system there, about the freedom young Norwegians enjoy, about the equality and justice and complete safety that prevails. Listening to him, I felt that this was the land I was seeking, a land where I dreamed of living out the years of my life.

"Can Iraqis get refugee status there?" I asked him.

"For sure. Norway loves and pampers Iraqis," he replied with confidence.

I didn't know, and had no way of knowing, whether he was telling the truth, especially when he spoke about

Norway's generosity towards the Iraqi community. But when he'd finished chewing the last of his sandwich, he told me that Norway was run by women, who outnumbered men five to one, and that these women loved Iraqi men, whom they saw as the epitome of Middle Eastern masculinity, and so they pampered them. Then, taking a scented handkerchief out of his pocket to wipe his hands and mouth, he said that Norwegian women melt like butter in a frying pan when they hold the hand of an Iraqi man. At that point the man's words made my knees wobble and my mouth salivate, so I kept it shut, pretending I had to change the oil in the pan.

17

"I want to emigrate," I told Salam one night.
"What? Emigrate? Where to?" he asked in surprise.
"To Norway."
"And why Norway in particular?"
"Because they love Iraqis."
At that Salam laughed hysterically.
"What are you laughing at?" I asked.
"I was laughing at the joke."
"What joke?"
"The joke about Norwegians loving Iraqis. Who on

earth told you that, for God's sake?"

"Never mind. Anyway, I've made up my mind to leave and that's that," I said.

Salam wasn't convinced by the sudden decision I had rolled out in front of him like a ball of wool, without any warning, so he kept on laughing. Maybe he was right to make fun of me, given that hasty, unplanned decisions shouldn't be taken seriously because the results are usually catastrophic. But when he noticed my tone of voice had changed, he had second thoughts and pulled his blanket over his head to go to sleep.

"So, you'd go abroad and leave me alone, you bastard?" he said.

"I have no other option, Salam. I'm fed up."

"Who are you fed up with, Said?"

"I'm fed up with being frightened and anxious and in suspense."

"Oof, all that!"

"Yes, all that and more. I escaped Baghdad, my friend, because I no longer felt safe there, and here I am, living with police raids every day. I want to move to a country where I feel safe. Understand?"

"Okay, okay. Let's sleep on it then and see what the morning brings."

18

I dived into the lake stark naked. What was the point of wearing clothes when the world was safe? But it was so cold my heart almost stopped. I cried out in shock. A blonde woman appeared out of nowhere and sprang towards me. She kissed me passionately on the lips, lighting a fire inside me till I felt warm. After a quick swim, we got out of the water, lit a fire and had sex beside it like cave people. After satisfying each other's desires, we put our clothes on and set off to climb up a white mountain. We agreed that the last one to the top would have to pull the sleigh. I beat her and won the challenge, but I spared her the task of pulling the sleigh. In other words, Arab gallantry still ran in my veins despite the snow. I had her sit down next to me, then I hitched the sleigh to four swift-footed wolfhounds. I loosened the reins and the dogs ran off towards the slope. The world looked like it was wearing a white wedding dress, and there was no limit to our delight, but one of the happy dogs tripped on a stone and the sleigh fell into the valley. I woke up to see a small, tailless mouse dancing on my chest.

19

"Don't forget to give my regards to Mister Harry," Hamza al-Amlat said as he dropped me off at the airport gate.

Hamza was in his thirties, clean-shaven with big green eyes and a complexion that showed signs of acne in the past. Salam had introduced me to him, saying he was the man who would take me to the other side of the world. We met in a small café on a street corner. He was quiet and had eyes that bulged, like someone watching a horror film in a dark cellar. We bargained with him over the money and gave him my passport with a passport photo. He examined them and said, "Great. Let's meet at the same time the day after tomorrow." When we met again, Hamza had my passport in his pocket, with a fake Slovenian visa on one of the pages. I paid him the money and he gave me the passport. He said a Serbian man called "Mister Harry" would be waiting for me there. and then he started to explain the plan, with names and dates. Salam had had to give up a large part of his savings for my sake and I had put that money with the money that I had and paid it over as the price for living under a safe roof one day.

My trip from Amman to Slovenia went through Moscow airport, and I was shaking like a wet palm frond in case I was found out. Standing in the queue behind an Iraqi woman and her young daughter, I held the girl's hand, and her mother smiled. At the time I felt that the woman was throwing me a massive lifeline. I handed my passport to the immigration officer straight after them, so that we would look like a family. The plan worked: the officer didn't notice that the visa was fake and he gave me the stamp that saved me. On the plane I thanked the woman with a nod and walked on to my seat. We arrived at Moscow airport about four hours later. A policeman with two stars on his shoulder was waiting for me at the plane door. He took my passport and said I would get it back as soon as I arrived in Slovenia. He said the same to the woman and her daughter and two young Palestinian men. They took us into a transit lounge and said we would have to wait there for seven hours, until the flight to Slovenia boarded. It was obvious this was a precautionary measure, to make sure we didn't leave the airport and seek asylum in Russia. When the plane landed at Ljubljana and we were about to disembark, the captain was standing at the door with our passports in an envelope in his hand. We took them and dispersed. I stopped a taxi and gave the driver the address of the hotel that Hamza had written on a small slip of paper, and he took me there.

After two nights of fear, anxiety and hunger in this

cheap hotel, Mister Harry, the promised Serbian trafficker, turned up. He was in his late forties, tall, burly and formidable. He spoke English badly. With help from his drawings on a cigarette packet, he said I had to leave the hotel at eight o'clock in the evening and head to a petrol station one kilometre north, then turn right and walk for twenty minutes and he'd be waiting for me there. I waited till eight, handed in my room key and left for the petrol station. There was no one there, and it looked like the place had been abandoned since the invention of tarmac. I turned right, following the sketch on the cigarette packet. After walking for twenty minutes along this unusual road, which looked like a rural road in the middle of a city, a truck in the distance flashed its headlights three times. That was the coded signal we had agreed at the hotel. I walked hurriedly towards the source of the light. It was a closed truck designed to carry frozen meat, with a picture of a fat calf on the side. I saw Mr Harry sitting in the front, next to the driver, whom he was later to call Assistant Conto. This Conto had a shaved head, lots of tattoos and a toothpick sticking out from the corner of his mouth, which he swivelled around like a radar scanner. I greeted him and he replied with a Mafia-style gesture, gesturing to the back door with his eyebrows. He followed me there, slid the bolt and signed to me to get on board. I climbed up like a prisoner-of-war who can do only what he is told. He closed the door with the bolt and a padlock and went back to the cabin.

As soon as I set foot in the truck, I know it would be an arduous and distressing journey. The inside of the truck was dark and there was a loud sound of breathing, interspersed with whisperings here and there. A smell of rotten meat lingered in the room, reminiscent of an unlicensed butcher's shop. I tripped over someone's leg and inadvertently apologised in Arabic, and in a low voice the person answered, "No problem. Come and sit down", also in Arabic, and tugged the hem of my jacket. He was a young Palestinian, probably no more than fifteen years old, anxiously biting his fingernails and speaking through clenched teeth. After I sat down next to him, he told me the police had stopped him twice before and put him in jail, and he didn't know if this route would be safe. "Shhh," whispered one of the other migrants. Apparently we were forbidden to chat until we reached the border. The truck drove five hours non-stop without any of us saying a word. Then it turned off, down a country road it seemed, that made it roll and sway for some time before it finally came to a stop. The back door opened and Mister Harry gestured that we should get down. He led us like sheep at Eid time towards a dilapidated building in the middle of an abandoned field. There were fifteen of us sheep, and fifteen others joined us from another truck. We emptied our bladders in the open, drank from some bottles of water and ate some fruit that one of the traffickers had brought. Half an hour later we resumed our journey on foot, a column of thirty migrants, led by Mister Harry and followed, a few paces behind, by a new colleague of his, whose name we did not know. They each had a small torch they used for signalling to each other: quick flashes meant "keep moving" and a steady light meant "stop". At least that's what I understood at the time.

After we'd walked for four miles without stopping, Mister Harry suddenly shouted "Go, go, go." From the way he waved his arm and the fact that he started running himself, we understood that he wanted us to run, too. We ran after him in panic because we didn't know what was happening around us or what the light approaching us was. Then Harry shouted "Stop" and we stopped. He signed that we should kneel on the ground, so we knelt. We were carrying out his orders like a flock of sheep obeying a shepherd. He put a finger to his lips and said, "Shhh." He had heard the sound of dogs approaching. A police patrol was searching the area. We held our breath and imagined what might be about to happen. I shut my eyes and held my mother's amulet. My heart almost froze in fear, because falling into the hands of the Slovakian police would mean spending the night behind bars. I opened my eyes to take a furtive look around. It was pitch black and everyone was holding their breath in fear and suspense, but the sound of the dogs had finally faded away, so the blood began to flow again in my veins. Mister Harry took out his torch and flashed a quick message to his colleague to say we should start walking again.

We continued to walk through the night, two abreast

like a military platoon. I was holding the hand of Mohammed the Palestinian, which was cold and shivering. I was trying to give him a sense of security that I lacked myself. Suddenly Mister Harry shouted "Go, go, go" and started running again. We ran behind him for two full hours and by the end of it I was almost dying of thirst. I let go of Mohammed's hand so as not to hamper his running, and fell back to the end of the column. Everyone but me was running briskly: I was out of breath and my ribs were killing me. I stopped and fell to the ground. I waved to the others and tried to shout "Stop! Stop!" but my voice was muffled and no one heard me. Then Harry's colleague noticed I had fallen behind and turned round to find me lying on the ground with my knees bleeding. He handed me a bottle of mineral water and helped me up. Then he took my hand and started pulling me along to catch up with the others. After another hour's non-stop running we ran into a chain-link fence held up by concrete posts with angled tops. Two trucks were waiting for us on the other side of the fence, not far off. Everyone managed to climb the fence nimbly except me: I was exhausted and unable to do it. I gave up and knelt on the ground like a stubborn camel. "Don't bother about me," I told Mohammed. "Leave me and go, please." But Mister Harry and his colleague came back to drag me and kick me to the other side. We got on the trucks and gathered from the way the traffickers were congratulating each other that we had crossed the Czech border and were now safe from the police.

The trucks drove us around for hours, and the smell in the truck was so bad that we took it in turns to stick our noses out of the small openings where fresh air came in. The truck smelled of rotten meat and farts and sweat from all the people inside. The place was like a giant sock that hadn't been washed since the First World War. We finally arrived at a large farm on the outskirts of Prague. We got down quietly and hid in an abandoned stable full of horseshit and mud, with rickety beds along both sides on which thousands of frightened bodies must have rested. At one end there was a dirty toilet, a washbasin and a table with worn edges, with some bread, fruit and small biscuits. We later found out that Harry's people-trafficking gang had chosen this place, which took shabbiness to the limit, as a centre for collecting migrants, and it was from here that a large convoy would set out for Germany. In the stable we found three Kurdish women aged between eighteen and twenty, an Afghan family of five, five young men from Kosovo, three Palestinians and two Iraqis who identified me before I could even sit down, as if I had a mark on my forehead showing I was their compatriot. The next day another group joined us, including many children, and in the end there were sixty-four of us migrants. Everyone had to stay indoors and keep quiet in case the farmers in the nearby fields informed on us. Meanwhile, Mister Harry and his colleagues drank alcohol in the trucks. We spent two rough nights in that stable before we received the signal to move on.

20

According to my new Iraqi companions, I was by this stage a pathetic sight. On the border between Slovakia and the Czech Republic I had thrown away my suitcase to save weight. When our journey resumed, I didn't have anything new to wear, unlike the others. Before we set off, everyone else put on the new clothes they had kept in their suitcases and left their dirty clothes behind in the stable. But I was coated in mud from head to toe and my shoes were leaking water through the holes that had opened up because of all the running. But I still insisted on completing the journey and making my way to a new home.

We formed a long line, with young men at the front and the back and the women in the middle. The group of sixty-four included two frightened Afghan girls. Two of the migrants volunteered to carry the girls so that they wouldn't hold up the convoy, while their mother watched them all the way. It wasn't just the girls who were frightened: everyone was trembling, because the Czech-German border was the most dangerous stage on the route we had followed. That's what Mister Harry said before the trip began. He explained to us in his laughable English, with occasional recourse to sign language, that the Czech police were active in the area and that anyone who fell into their hands would be locked up or deported. The rough terrain and the darkness added to the danger. It was cold and there were snow drifts here and there.

As we walked, the only light we saw was from the traffickers' torches, whether steady or flashing. We walked ten miles through snow and darkness, and I felt as if my feet had frozen and I was bound to get frostbite. "O God, will my feet be the price I pay for getting to Norway?" I said to myself as I knelt like a camel from the intense pain. But one of the traffickers told me off, like someone shouting at a dog that's approaching some food. He grabbed my arm and tried to make me stand. With his help I walked on, gritting my teeth to distract from the pain. Moments later we heard dogs barking. Mister Harry turned off his torch and told us to stop and lie flat on the ground until the police patrol had passed. I buried my face in the snow, cursing the fates that had brought me into this world and wondering why safety was so unfairly distributed on our planet. Why did people have to suffer in order to move from one side of the world to another? Who had reduced me to this state? How had my future come to depend on either a drunken trafficker or the merciless border police? What other surprises did the world have in store for me? Questions that wouldn't have ended were it not for the flashing light from Mister Harry's torch.

But it all passed peacefully and the Czech dogs didn't sniff us out. This was no doubt a mistake that history would hold against the stupid dogs, because we smelled so bad that they should have been able to smell us from a thousand miles away. After a few minutes lying in the snow we walked on, but this time the leader's instincts had misled him: the dogs were not as stupid as we had thought and the Czech police had set up an ambush behind some snow-covered trees. Improvisation was now the best response to the new situation, especially as Mister Harry, when he noticed the ambush, had jabbered some incomprehensible instructions. We fled left and right, skipping like sheep pursued by dogs so ravenous they must have been waiting two years for such prey. Barking dogs brought down one man and bit another as they chased us, rubbing our dignity in the mud. After two hours of this unequal pursuit, we found that the number of people in our group had shrunk to only twenty and the others had vanished – either lost in the forests and the snow or captured by the Czech police. I was among the survivors, along with Mister Harry and his colleagues, who had found a way to escape from the ambush. We gathered on a densely wooded hill and the traffickers tried to work out who had made it. We were surprised to find that the Afghan family was not among our group of survivors, while their young daughters were still being carried on the shoulders of two tall traffickers. We urged Mister Harry to go back and look for their parents, but he wouldn't go, saying they had probably been caught by the Czech police. Then he took a bottle of beer out of his coat pocket, proceeded to empty it down his throat, wiped his moustache and mercilessly shouted, "Let's go!"

We walked after him like mourners at a funeral, to the sobbing of the Afghan girls, who might as well have been orphans at this stage. We crossed the border and got into two trucks that were waiting for us on German territory. The agreement was that Mister Harry would take us to Hanover, and from there we would each go our own way. The trucks took us to the outskirts of Hanover, and dropped us off along the way, one by one so as not to arouse suspicion. Harry kept me till the end, along with the two Afghan girls and Mohammed the Palestinian. He stopped the truck outside an isolated house surrounded by trees and slipped a piece of paper into my hand with a message written in English. "Three miles north towards Hanover train station," it read. He told us to get out, so we got out, and the two girls were shaking in fear. Mohammed took to his heels, while I stayed put to face my future with two lost girls who were good for nothing but crying. I picked one of them up and held the other's hand, and just stood there, not knowing what to do. I had landed myself in serious trouble and thought I would end up rotting away behind bars in a German jail on a charge of child smuggling. But something unexpected stirred at the door to the house. I put down the girl I was carrying on my shoulder, told her sister to hold her hand, and then slipped behind a lamp post a few yards away to see what would happen. The door opened and a very old woman came out, her thin body wrapped in a white cotton dressing gown. Her back bent, the woman hobbled slowly towards the post box. She noticed the girls standing at the gate and hurried towards them. She bent down to ask them a question that I couldn't hear, then put her arms around them and took them inside. I breathed a sigh of relief and the blood flowed again in my veins. I had dealt with that problem and felt confident that the girls would be safe. The kind old woman would no doubt call the police, who would find a solution. I set off towards the main railway station, where I was meant to meet a stocky man in a grey suit, with a black woollen hat and a black backpack carrying the Nike logo.

21

Twenty-four years earlier Ayoub Ghazal had arrived in Hanover and met a German woman who owned a hamburger restaurant. They married and he took over management of the restaurant after adding the word halal on the front window. But he didn't just serve halal hamburgers: he was also in the business of smuggling people, cigarettes and cheap beer. We arrived at his place and he pointed me to the upper floor. We went upstairs and there was just a small bathroom and a large room for the workers. He said I should wash and change my clothes, because the way I looked was suspicious. I washed and put on the clean suit and shirt that Ayoub had given me and a pair of trainers of the kind sold in cheap shops. I looked in the mirror to arrange my hair. I looked like a goat that had done some serious running. "What's up with you, Said? Have you just completed a marathon for hungry goats?" I asked the mirror. In the meantime, I could hear my stomach rumbling from hunger, so I left the mirror to itself and went downstairs. One of the restaurant workers served me a hamburger that looked delicious. I gestured that I was still hungry, so he added a plate of chips.

In Amman Hamza al-Amlat had told me that as soon as I met Ayoub Ghazal at the station, he would arrange for me to reach Norway. He claimed that Ayoub's task was the easiest part of the journey, since it meant simply arranging a lift on a truck to Kiel in the far north of Germany and then a boat trip to Oslo. But Ayoub had other ideas. After giving me new clothes and satisfying my hunger, he took me to a small flat in a building near the restaurant and told me he would come back that evening. He didn't keep his promise, of course, but when do traffickers ever keep their promises? The flat I was in was cold, damp and badly ventilated, on the third floor of a dodgy building inhabited by druggies and weed dealers. When I went inside, I saw piles of cardboard boxes and crates of smuggled beer. Then I was surprised to find a Kurdish family of five leaning against each other like a line of dominoes and two young Syrians blowing cigarette smoke in each other's faces. Everyone was waiting for Ayoub to feel sorry for them and send them on to safe havens. There was nowhere to sleep and the flat wasn't a place to relax. Everything around me made me anxious. At about nine in the evening, a flashing blue light appeared outside and I saw a police car at the entrance to the building, followed by another vehicle that disgorged strapping policemen armed with truncheons. "So that's the end of that, Said," I said through gritted teeth, pulling back from the window so that none of the policemen would see me.

"What's up? Why have you gone so pale?" asked one of the Syrians.

"Shh, police, police," I replied, putting a finger to my lips.

I was frightened the police had come looking for migrants and we would fall into their hands. So I bolted the door on the inside and asked the people in the flat to keep quiet. But the sound of boots went past us up to the fourth floor, and I let out a long sigh. Evidently, we weren't the targets of this raid, but rather the drug dealers. From behind the window I saw the police put three of them into the back of their truck. The next day

Ayoub came to tell us our trip was delayed and we would have to wait a whole week. He didn't give a good reason for the delay and didn't waste his time explaining. People traffickers are not usually interested in the questions that bother the heads of migrants. All he said was that we had to wait till the danger passed.

I took out my wallet and counted the dollars I had left. "How much do you think it would cost to reach Kiel?" I asked one of the Syrians.

"Have you decided to go there alone?" he replied.

"Yes. Do you want to come with me?"

"It's a good idea. What do you say, Shadi?" he said, glancing at his friend.

The other man seemed to like the idea. "So, we'll leave together," he said.

We agreed we wouldn't stay in Ayoub's flat another hour. The man was apparently a time-waster who used the flat as a storeroom for cigarettes, beer and migrants. He clearly gave priority to his own financial interests and intended to assemble as many migrants as possible so that he could make more money on the trip. We decided to leave immediately. We were encouraged in our decision by Shadi's ability to communicate because of his previous work as an English teacher in Aleppo. So we made our way to Hanover train station. There weren't any policemen or patrols there to check people's identity papers, as we had assumed there would be. All we saw was a ticket clerk in a suit with the logo of the German railways, smiling behind the screen at the ticket office, and travellers with suitcases waiting for trains on the platforms. Shadi walked towards the ticket counter confidently but, just before he got there, he caught sight of a burly policeman coming into the station with a dog in tow. He panicked and retraced his steps. He came back to us trembling in fear and completely tongue-tied. If we hadn't left the station quickly, we would have been found out and would have ended up as the guests of that unexpected policeman.

We went back to Ayoub in his restaurant and threatened to inform the German authorities of his activities and show them the way to his flat if he didn't arrange for us to leave for Kiel immediately. He finally gave in to our threats and told us to wait for him at a café three streets away while he got himself ready. An hour and twenty minutes later he turned up in his small green van, with the name of his restaurant on the side, and told us to get in. I sat next to him in the front while the Syrians sat with the clutter in the back, and off we drove to Kiel. The man didn't say a word throughout the journey, until we reached the port about three hours later. He said the boat right in front of us would sail for Oslo in twenty-five minutes and the next boat would go to Gothenburg in Sweden, according to the noticeboard. I was the only one planning to go to Oslo. Ayoub booked me a ticket and told me where to embark. "Make sure you don't look back and arouse any suspicions," he added. My Syrian companions who had decided to go to Sweden had to wait for the next boat.

I said goodbye to them and went aboard the massive white and blue ferry, which was flying the Norwegian flag. After twenty hours at sea, we reached Oslo.

22

Alone in Oslo like an orphan, I walked along Storgata Street. I didn't know where to go to register as a refugee in the Kingdom of Norway. Although it was in the city centre, the street wasn't crowded and the ratio of women to men wasn't as outrageously imbalanced as that rosy-cheeked young man in Amman had led me to believe. Even when I looked into a woman's eyes, on the pretext of asking directions, they didn't seem interested in me. When I put out my hand to thank them, they certainly didn't melt like butter in a frying pan, to use his expression, although I have a face that a blind chicken in the Himalayas, if asked, could instantly identify as that of an Iraqi born of Iraqi parents.

I stopped outside a department store with the name Gunerius in blue lights across the facade. I walked inside aimlessly and examined the goods in the display cabinets and went out of another door. I saw someone standing behind a fancy cart, with leather belts and colourful thick woollen socks hanging from the awning. On the cart itself lay fur hats and gloves made of deerskin and lined with fur. I bought one of those thick hats that Inuit reindeer herders wear and walked on down a narrow street behind the shopping centre. It had Asian and African grocery shops, with goods on display outside on wooden tables with little price signs. I carried on down the street till I reached a restaurant with a big glass window on which the words *Halal Kebabs* had been written in Arabic. "Welcome, fellow speakers of Arabic!" I whispered to myself. I went inside and said hello. A thin young man with a Yemeni accent returned my greeting. He was busy making a tray of kebabs the Turkish way. I waited till he'd finished, then asked him the way to the police station.

"Are you a new refugee?" he said with a smile.

"Yes, but how did you know?"

"Because here the only people who ask the way to the police station are the ones seeking asylum," he explained.

"Ah, so that's how it is!"

"Yes, it is."

"So where would I find it, if you don't mind?"

"Never mind, you're here now. First, tell me, have you had lunch?"

"I ate on the way, thanks."

The man offered me a cup of tea and volunteered to take me to the police station. We went out of the restaurant and turned right. We walked some distance, then turned left and stopped a few steps further. He pointed at a tall building and hurried off, worried he might be accused of people trafficking. It was a six-storey government building with large tinted windows. At the door there was a brass plaque with the crest of the Norwegian police.

I stood alone outside this formidable building, shivering from both fear and cold. I pressed the bell cautiously, like someone prodding a sleeping lion. The door opened automatically and I went inside. I found myself in front of a small desk with a well-dressed woman sitting behind it. She asked me what language I spoke and where I was from. "Arabic, from Iraq," I said. She handed me a small piece of paper and gestured that I should write out my name in Latin characters. I wrote it out and then she asked me to put my thumb on an illuminated screen that photographed my thumbprint. After that, I stepped aside to wait for further instructions. The woman picked up the telephone and spoke to someone in a language I didn't understand. The only word I could make out was Iraq. A policeman with rippling muscles appeared, as tall as a sleepless night is long. He took me deeper into the building and left me in a large hall with a high ceiling. There were men, women and children lying on the floor like tired puppies. Illegal immigrants, as the affluent world likes to call them. People on the run from injustice, persecution, hunger and pointless wars. Some of them had come by sea, wrapped in the torn remnants of tents, some of them had crossed borders hiding at the bottom of wooden crates, and others had walked thousands of miles to reach this hall, which was full of diversity. I spent the time counting the stories of fear and humiliation etched on their faces: this man was on the run from religious militias that assassinated those who disobeyed, this man from a brutal war that didn't want to end, this man and his children from a famine that the power-brokers hadn't noticed, that woman from patriarchal tyranny and oppression. As for that man hiding in the corner, he was tired of not having a homeland, so he moved away to find one.

In the evening we formed a long queue at the back door of the building and a white bus came to pick us up, driven by a veteran migrant who now worked for the immigration department. We were taken to a refugee reception centre and given identity cards with numbers instead of names. My number was 777, and from then on they called me seven-seven-seven. I didn't really care what they called me. As long as I had a warm bed in a safe country, there was no harm in being three sevens, or nine fives, or even an insignificant zero for that matter. In the past I had had many names, but they hadn't kept me warm. My mother, for example, had called me Said, which means "happy", but I was fatherless and hapless and I'd never seen happiness in my life. The city where I was born gave me the nickname Ibn Dar al-Salam, Son of the Abode of Peace, originally Baghdad's official name, but I grew up afraid, seeing one war end only for another war to flare up, more brutal and more ugly than the previous one. History had given me many nicknames, such as Son of Mesopotamia, Grandson of Gilgamesh, and Nephew of Hammurabi, but all I gained from those names was disappointment and despair. One of the refugees sat next of me and complained that he was number 111. "What the hell is that?" he said, "They've turned us into numbers, man! God curse them." "What you should really say is 'God curse those who are the reason we're here', Mister One-One-One," I whispered in his ear. Then we had an argument over who most deserved to be cursed and we raised our voices, but we soon realised that cursing wouldn't restore our lost names and we would spend the rest of our lives as meaningless numbers on lists of refugees, and we calmed down.

After twenty-three days in the refugee reception centre a young man came from the immigration department with an Arabic translator. He introduced himself and then asked me to follow them. He said he was called Markus and he was going to give me a long interview to decide if I qualified for refugee status. I said goodbye to my friend One-One-One, and went off with them. I followed Markus to the third floor of the building like an obedient puppy. Asylum seekers are as obedient as little dogs: the examiners and their translators know this well. We walked down a long corridor, then turned right to a special room with closed, tinted windows. The young interrogator was rigorous and kept springing unexpected questions on me until I felt that my skull was about to crack and I almost threw up in front of him.

23

I stopped on the side of the road, opened the car door and vomited. Then I took out a bottle of mineral water, rinsed my face with it and drank what was left. I finished sorting the mail in the rain and went back home soaked in water, my head full of memories. I arrived exhausted. I got undressed and stood under the shower, trying to douse the flames burning in my head. The doctor once advised me to give up working for the postal service because it was stressful work and gave me constant headaches, but I didn't listen to him. Finding a new job was like winning the lottery: it would take great patience and good luck that I didn't possess.

In fact, I had never thought I'd become a postman and I hadn't planned it in the least. If it hadn't been for my mother and her need for money, I would have done without the job and gone back to studying literature. It wouldn't be hard to find a place in one of the many Norwegian universities up and down the country. What did I care for the postal service? How had my dream of writing died, burnt to ashes in the furnace that is life? How had a silly joke ruined my life and made my days as dark as an abandoned dungeon? I turned off the shower and came out naked. I turned off my mobile phone and took the landline receiver off the hook so that no one could disturb me. Then I swallowed a sleeping pill and sank into bed.

24

Three days after my asylum interview, news came that the list of people assigned to permanent centres had arrived and had been pinned up on the noticeboard by the door. At the time they were chosen at random, so luck played a large role in it. I went to the noticeboard and found that bad luck was still pursuing me. I was to be dumped in the town of Alta in the far north of the country, where the winters would be very cold and dark. I flew there two days later with eight other refugees who were either Arabs or Kurds. When we reached our new accommodation, the manager told us it was going to snow for three nights, with snow more than two metres deep, and the temperature would fall to -30 Celsius. "Woe is you, Said!" I wailed when I heard him. "It's too early for wailing, man," replied the person standing next to me.

Our accommodation was a large house with eight bedrooms, in a village four miles from the town centre.

At Rest in the Cherry Orchard

The roof was covered in snow and the building as a whole was in poor condition. The stove devoured small logs with the appetite of a wolf and its mouth gaped until the morning, demanding more. We were each assigned to one of eight small bedrooms and I ended up sharing with a refugee from Sudan who had arrived three months before me. They nicknamed him Othman Couldn't-Care-Less. I remember that one evening, just to make conversation, I said to him, "You know what? Living below zero is a slow death."

But he didn't reply. He just pouted without saying a single word. After I had tried eighty-five times to draw him into conversation, he finally waved his hand in the air as if trying to swat a fly and said, "I don't care." Then he returned to his silence. He was eccentric, but I continued to chip away at his wall of silence till I loosened his tongue. He said he was a refugee with a long history of seeking asylum. He had fled Sudan to Egypt and left for Libya two years later. Then he sailed to Italy on a rickety old boat. He stayed in Italy only a year, though he found easy work there. He worked as a cowherd on a farm owned by a fat Italian woman who hired him for two tasks – to graze her cows by day and sleep with her at night. He swore he was telling the truth, letting out one sigh after another. After a year in this cushy job, as he called it, someone tipped off the Italian police that he didn't have a work permit, and he had to go on the run. He escaped the farm before the police arrived and moved from town to town. In the end he met an Arab family that was driving around Italy on holiday. He told them his sad story and they brought him to Norway, where they were living, sometimes in the boot of their car. Whenever they were about to cross a border they stopped to let him hide in the boot until they were safely through to the other side. He laughed as he told the story and when I asked him how he could talk about his harrowing ordeal with such detachment he said he was so used to being kicked in the arse that he no longer cared.

One day I told him we didn't have anything to eat and we had to go to the shop to buy some bread. But he refused to come with me, saying it was pitch black in the village and the street was covered in snow and slippery. It wasn't far to the only shop in the village, but he had grown so lazy he wouldn't come with me. He said repeatedly that life wasn't worth so much trouble and that no one ever died of hunger, but I blocked my ears to avoid hearing the litany of despair he had perfected, and out I ventured. I found the village was indeed pitch dark and the snow that the snowplough had moved had left a layer of ice on the asphalt that was hard to walk on. I checked the thermometer at the door and it read -32 degrees Celsius. I could feel the cold air pricking my face like pins and after just a few steps I lost all sensation in my nose and mouth. Gradually the tears I had shed because of the cold froze on my eyelashes and my cheeks, while my moustache turned as stiff as twigs in a broom. I looked back and saw Othman behind the window pane, waving at me to come back, which made me even more determined to complete my mission. With great difficulty and extreme caution I made my way across the ice. I had almost reached the shop when I slipped and fell. The paramedics wrote down the damage: a broken hand, a lost tooth and an empty stomach. That day I swore I would leave that town even if gold fell from the sky instead of snow. When I had fully recovered, I packed my bag and flew back to Oslo.

25

I didn't yet speak Norwegian very well and no one was waiting for me at the arrivals gate. In the distance I spotted a public telephone standing close to the ticket machine. I headed towards it, inserted an international phone card and dialled home in Baghdad. My mother picked up the phone and bombarded me with questions. I could hear the anxiety in her voice and it tore at my heartstrings. But somehow I felt a kind of security that is hard to explain. I said goodbye, ended the conversation and walked out towards the smoking room.

"Sayyed, Sayyed!" someone shouted behind me.

I turned and found a traveller holding my bag.

"Ah, I'd forgotten it. Thank you," I said.

"Are you Arab?" the man asked with a smile.

"Yes, I'm Iraqi," I replied.

"Pleased to meet you. I'm Rachid from Morocco," he said.

At that moment I felt that the fates were throwing me a lifeline.

"You don't look well. Are you okay?" asked Rachid.

"No, I'm not ill," I said. "Just lost," I added with a long deep sigh.

We went into the smoking room. He offered me a light and said, "What would you say to working with me in a workshop that dismantles old cars?"

I agreed without hesitation. We bought two tickets and got on the train from the airport to the city centre. Oslo was almost deserted because of the cold weather that had struck. We ate doner kebab at a small Turkish restaurant and went out towards the metro station. From there we took the train to the Stovner district, where the workshop was. It was a garage surrounded by a high concrete wall, full of scrap metal, with two caravans on the right-hand side. The large one, which was slowly falling apart, was a dormitory for the workers, and the smaller one was an office for sales and administration. On the other side there was a third caravan where they stored good pieces of scrap that had been recovered.

Rachid bought up old cars and took them to pieces to recover whatever could be sold as spares. The rest went to the smelters to be melted down and recycled. Breaking up the cars was tiring work and the caravan I slept in after long hours at work wasn't fit for human habitation. It was a damp, cramped box, putrid and unhygienic. It had a wooden bunk bed for two. Morten, an immigrant from Kosovo, slept on the top bunk. He may have been stupid but he was world-class at snoring and smelling bad. He washed only once a millennium and it didn't bother him if strange sounds came out of his various orifices while he slept. I laughed often on the first night as I listened to this disaster in the bed above me, but I also cried, because I didn't get to sleep till morning. But as the days passed I came to the conclusion that a mixture of laughing and crying shows that the world is quite absurd and the only option is to go with the flow, and that is what I did.

One night a snowstorm blew up that made the caravan feel like a massive freezer for frozen fish. The temperature fell to -23 degrees Celsius and the heating system broke down. My ribs began to shake from the cold and my teeth chattered like crazy. I lit a small heater that we had and covered myself with two miserable blankets and a tacky duvet that hundreds of people had used before me. I managed to get some warmth into my bones and nodded off, but it didn't last long. I was awoken by what felt like an earthquake: I never could find out how it rated on the Richter scale. The bed was shaking violently and Morten's heavy breathing was audible through my covers despite the howling wind. I stuck my head out from under the filthy blankets to find that disaster had struck us. Morten was awake and masturbating with enthusiasm. The idiot couldn't find anywhere better to ejaculate than over my head. Then he sat down with me for breakfast in the morning before even washing his hands. At that stage I left the rest of the food untouched and said, "You finish off. I'm full. I'll start work before you."

"Okay, okay, my friend," he said, stuffing a whole boiled egg in his mouth and swallowing it down like a hungry snake.

Morten had come to Norway four years earlier as a refugee from Kosovo after an unsuccessful experience in Germany. He hadn't intended to come to the snow kingdom, as he called it, but he had to after the German authorities rejected his asylum request and decided to send him back to his country. At the last moment he gave the German policeman deporting him the slip. He told the policeman his bladder was about to burst and the policeman stopped the car at a mobile toilet on the road and he escaped. He ran up a hill covered in pine trees and stayed in hiding till late at night. Early the next morning, with help from a kindly farmer, he boarded a train to Copenhagen, and then went on to Norway by sea. His request for asylum in Norway was also rejected, because of the records that the German authorities had, so ever since he'd been in hiding and working in Rachid's scrapyard. Morten told me the story of his travels one thousand, nine hundred and ninety-one times until I remembered it as well as fathers remember their daughters' names. Every time I heard his story, I had a panic attack for fear I might meet the same fate as him.

In fact, the snow kingdom had not rejected my asylum request and no one had decided to deport me, but I was afraid and I tried to avoid Morten whenever he started telling his story. Every morning I would ask Rachid if there was any mail for me and he would say no, leaving me at the mercy of my stupid colleague in a caravan that wasn't fit for human habitation. But this didn't last long. One day the Norwegian police raided the scrapyard in full force to arrest and deport Morten. One of our customers had tipped them off after a disagreement with Rachid.

26

One cold morning I picked up an electric chainsaw and went to work on a Mercedes S350. It was a new car but the owner had had to sell it as scrap after smashing it up in an accident. I took off the rear tyres for resale and dismantled the trunk. Then I turned the car upside down and started to remove the good parts of the body, using the saw and spanners. Then I put labels on all the good parts to make it easier to identify them later. Finally, I painted red paint on the parts that were scrap and took the good parts to the warehouse. I put everything in its right place and went back to start work on another car. Meanwhile, Rachid turned up with the shoulder bag in which he usually put a small packed lunch and some work documents. He called me over, opened the bag and handed me a white envelope with the logo of the Norwegian immigration department. I opened the envelope warily. It was a long letter in Norwegian and my Norwegian wasn't good enough for me to read it easily. But a word often used on special occasions stood out on the first line: Gratulerer.

"Rachid, it's a congratulations letter. What does it mean?" I asked.

Rachid took the letter and read it quickly to himself. I felt that good news was on its way. Rachid opened his arms and shouted, "Congratulations, Said. You have asylum in Norway." I hugged him and wept.

At last I had another home, thank God! At last I had the right to feel safe. At last I would no longer shake in fear whenever there was a knock on the door, a feeling known to everyone who has lived through the terror in Iraq. We would jump whenever we heard violent knocking on the door, because in those days night-time raids usually meant you'd be dragged off to the cells and disappear.

The next day Rachid lent me a large dictionary and some notebooks he said would be of great use to me in language school. "Rest assured, I'll devour Norwegian like Morten devours eggs," I said, and we laughed.

27

A blonde woman, twenty-six years old, tall with unusual dimples, eyes as blue as the North Sea and breasts as prominent as the Bergen mountains, put out her hand to shake mine at the door to the classroom and said she was the language teacher, Tona Jensen, and would be with us for the whole year. She was kinder than anyone else I've ever known. Some women cannot be gratuitously likened to any other woman because they are unique and incomparable in themselves. The goodness and kindness of this particular woman always amazed me, and made me suspect she was made of pure honey.

I attended the language classes conscientiously, arriving early like a diligent student. To be honest I wasn't interested in subjects and objects or diphthongs and how to pronounce them. All that mattered to me was winning a smile from Tona that would give me pleasure. One day she stood at the board explaining pronouns and the difference in pronunciation and meaning between the Norwegian words *du* and *do*. I was daydreaming at the time and my mind was somewhere else, but not far away, just on her lower lip in fact, giving free rein to an innate imagination that made up stories with uninhibited freedom. In the meantime, she ambushed me, God forgive her, by asking me to put the first word, which just means 'you', into a sentence. "Said, Said, Said," she said, but to no avail. I was lost in the world of lips. I could see her speaking but I couldn't hear her. "Saiiiid," she shouted, and I came to my senses. "Yes, yes, Miss Tona, go ahead," I said. "Come here please and put the word *du* in a sentence," she continued. Embarrassed, I walked to the blackboard, took the chalk from her hand and wrote "*Jeg elsker do*" in large letters. Everyone laughed aloud at me and Miss Tona almost fell to the floor laughing. Surprised, I smiled at them blankly, without understanding the joke. It later transpired that my sentence meant "I love toilet", when what I meant to write was "*Jeg elsker du*" or "I love you".

I fell in love with that woman and when I'd learnt to put words together in Norwegian, I called her *Honning Slurk*, or Honeysip. She laughed whenever I called her that and pointed out that she didn't like honey. The massive differences between languages sometimes get me into trouble, especially when other people don't understand what this or that reference means. Once I said "You're an apple" to a girl on the underground and she looked terrified I might pounce on her and try to eat her. Once I was at a meeting with a civil servant in some government department and I said, "You're pretty. You have cheeks like pomegranates." When she heard that, she stood up, went to a small fridge in her office, opened it and said, "Sorry, I don't have any pomegranates, as you can see. Would grapes do?" She thought I wanted a pomegranate right there and then.

At the end of our first lesson, Honeysip asked us to write a two-page essay on any subject we chose, to test our ability to express ourselves. I remember writing four pages about cross-fertilisation between civilisations, multi-ethnic societies and how people integrate. I finished off the essay with a desperate attempt to catch her with a fish hook: "A scion of Mesopotamian civilisation dreams about inviting his beautiful teacher, a scion of the Viking civilisation, to a cup of coffee in his home, but he suspects, may God disprove his suspicions, that the accursed fates are lying in wait to thwart this noble dream." But what happened that day was a complete surprise. The fish took the bait, I don't know why, and the hook caught. Miss Tona came after me and said, "Give me your address, Said, and I'll come on Saturday evening, to make sure that the fates don't thwart your noble dreams."

28

I picked up the clothes scattered here and there and put them in the washing machine. I washed the pots and pans that had piled up in the kitchen sink over the previous two days. I gathered the books and magazines that were lying around. I vacuum-cleaned the sitting room, tidied up the stuff on the television and sat down thinking where I should receive my guest when she came the next day. In the sitting room? On the balcony? Would we need the bedroom? Would Tona go into the kitchen to cook us some food after a long bout of cuddling? But then, would we really get to have a cuddle, or was the programme for the visit limited to debating the cross-fertilisation of civilisations? Maybe there was no need to worry, because the rare stroke of luck that made the hook catch would surely have a lasting effect and would take me beyond just a friendly conversation. First, I would invite her to smoke shisha on the balcony and drink some sweet Iraqi tea there, instead of bitter Norwegian coffee. Sweetness is essential on romantic nights. Then I'd take her into the sitting room to offer her some fine red wine, and white wine too, since I didn't know which she preferred. In Baghdad we weren't in the habit of drinking wine. Arak dominated the scene in drinking establishments, but changing your drink is an essential part of integrating into alternative countries. Beside the wine on the table I would place some mezes that go with wine. This time I would make no compromises: the mezes would be Arab and to hell with integration. Without an Arab meze, drinks have no savour and the drinkers won't enjoy themselves properly. I would simmer the chickpeas, squeeze two lemons onto them with a generous pinch of salt. Next to the hummus, I'd have a bowl of tabbouleh and a bowl of jajeek, and nuts from Kaka Sirvan. I would buy walnuts, almonds, pistachios and hazelnuts from him, and wonderful oriental nuts of every kind. I certainly wouldn't forget potato chips, olives and a romantic film to light up our evening.

Okay, I have to go now, I told myself, adjusted my clothes and went out. I bought the meze ingredients from Kaka Sirvan and passed by a nearby shop that sells DVDs to ask the saleswoman for a film suitable for a small party for a potential new love interest.

"Please, could you recommend a film with some nice romantic scenes?" I asked.

"Mmm, it sounds like you have a hot date," she replied with a smile.

"Yes, very hot, very hot, very, very," I kept repeating like a broken record.

"Okay, take this. It might have what you're looking for," she said, hoping to keep me quiet.

I took the DVD from her and went back to my flat. I sat on the sofa and looked at the picture of the actress on the cover. Tona would be there the next day. I'd turn off the lights and put on the film. I'd watch her out of the corner of my eye as the actress sighed in the embrace of the hero, their hands intertwined. Who knows? Maybe my guest would rest her head on my shoulder or slip her hand into mine or sigh like the woman in the film. But when the film was over and the bottle of wine was drunk, what would happen? Would my guest ask me to carry her into the bedroom? Or would she stand up and dance with me, then lose concentration and slump against my chest, for me to carry her there? I don't know, I don't know. But first I had to sally forth to clean up the bedroom. Then I could come back and reimagine the scene.

I took off the old sheet and put on one that was fit for Tona: she might not like the smell of the old one. I opened the window, something I hadn't done in two months. Bachelors always keep their windows closed. I swept the floor and set up two scented candles. Scented candles are essential on such evenings, playing two roles in one: the delicate scent and the soft light. When these are combined, people unwind, according to Mansoura Qaddouf, one of my colleagues at the language school.

She was an Eritrean woman who spoke Arabic in a funny way, using masculine pronouns instead of the feminine and vice versa, using plurals instead of singulars and singulars instead of duals.

Whenever she spoke Arabic to me, I suggested she leave the Arabic aside and speak Norwegian instead. "That'd be easier for both of us," I added. Even so, she wouldn't stop giving me advice, saying that men should set aside a small amount of their salaries to buy scented candles, because they were so indescribably magical. She swore solemn oaths to this. After she'd given me her advice, I asked, "And does your husband unwind when he sees you doing that?"

"I don't know, but when he smells them, he does his man-thing with me and goes to sleep."

For a moment I thought I didn't care whether my guest felt love or desire, since the two would mean much the same to a bachelor living in a building alongside hundreds of old people. But I soon drove this primitive idea out of my head when I remembered who the guest would be. It was Tona Jensen, the beloved whom fate had thankfully held in store for me.

The next day I stood back and took a last look at my completed preparations. "Great, everything's wonderful. The only thing left is having a shower," I said to myself. I threw my clothes off and went under the shower. The warm water was as welcome as ever, but this time I wasn't so interested in it and I didn't feel the same pleasure as usual when I have a hot shower. Like anyone waiting for someone to arrive, my mind was unconsciously on the door, and I was anticipating Tona's arrival, although it was still early. I turned off the shower tap and went out. I poured the remains of a bottle of scent on my body, put on a pristine shirt, then lit the scented candles and sat down on the balcony to watch the bus arrive. My god, how slowly time passes when you're waiting!

29

As I watched out for Tona from the balcony, I remembered one night when I came home late. There weren't any passengers on the bus at the time and I was sitting in the back seats while the driver hummed along to some loud pop music on the radio. The bus stopped at one stop and a man got on, wearing a black woollen coat, high boots and a large black fur hat. He sat behind the driver. The bus went two stops without anyone else getting on. It was rather late. I switched on the light above my head and busied myself reading a book. I looked up and saw that the strange man was bleeding from behind his ears and blood was running down over his shoulders. I rubbed my eyes in the hope of seeing more clearly. He really was bleeding and his blood was pouring down onto the floor and slowly filling the bus. I found it hard to breathe. The man turned towards me and I saw it was my father. He came up to me and removed the blood-stained bandage from his face, but the bus ran into a metal wall, the windows broke and my father disappeared. I came around to find I had fallen asleep on the bus and missed my stop.

30

I took her coat from her, smelled it and kissed it without her seeing, then hung it on the hanger behind the door. I breathed in her fragrance and felt dizzy. As I followed her into the sitting room, she said my flat was beautiful. I nodded and smiled, grateful for the compliment. I invited her to sit on the balcony first because I'd arranged chairs there so that we could start work on the cross-fertilisation of our two civilisations – Mesopotamia and the Vikings. In the middle stood a Baghdad-style shisha in turquoise glass topped by a ceramic bowl stuffed with a tobacco mixture flavoured with grapes that had been fermenting since the Six Day War in 1967. On top of the bowl rested two burning coals, as red as rubies. Nearby stood a table with a samovar that gave off the smell of cardamom tea, and gilt teacups as elegant as Anatolian dolls.

"My god, what's all this, Said!" said Tona. "It's like a throne room," I replied with a wink "I prepared it for the most beautiful teacher in Scandinavia. Come and sit down." My guest laughed and winked back at me. I was confident things were going in the right direction and that my stroke of luck would last this time.

My guest had never smoked a shisha before, so she found it hard at the first try. But I told her that smoking a shisha was easier than clapping and all she had to do was inhale the smoke and enjoy it in her lungs. After only half an hour, Tona was taking a drag, and holding it in her lungs for a while before exhaling. Then she would pass me the shisha, following the venerable etiquette for shishas. The nicest thing was that we were passing the pipe back and forth without me changing the mouthpiece. It would be stupid to change the mouthpiece when you're sharing a shisha with a woman. The taste of the smoke changed after Tona had taken two puffs, and tasted like grapes with honey. After that the walls of inhibition collapsed one after another, and we started laughed loudly in clouds of smoke. I was telling her stupid jokes but she was laughing more at my broken Norwegian than at the jokes themselves. I told her seven thousand jokes and five hundred and fifty funny stories until I thought she was going to die laughing. To her I must have sounded like Mansoura Qaddouf sounded to me when she babbled away in Arabic. We laugh when we hear a foreigner speaking our language incorrectly. Only people who speak the same language don't laugh at each other when they converse. In the end she asked me to stop telling jokes because her stomach muscles were hurting, so I complied out of deference to her health. After that we went into the sitting room to watch the film that the woman in the shop had recommended. Tona smiled when she read the title on the screen: *A Warm Bed*. I winked as I poured her a glass of red wine, and then a second and a third until I felt that the devil had indeed turned up as the third in our gathering and was welcome and that everything was going to plan. The film was about to end and the romantic scenes had left their mark on Tona's face. She leaned flirtatiously on my shoulder and pointed at the bed. "Forward march," she said. I planted a kiss on her mouth, as an appetizer, then picked her up and carried her off like a triumphant soldier. I put her down on the bed gently, unbuttoned her blouse and started to undress her, one garment at a time. I devoured her lips, then planted kisses on her neck and breasts, then moved down to between her legs. She grabbed me by my hair, wrapped her legs around me and we spent the night locked together. In the morning I woke up to find she'd gone, leaving a small scrap of paper on the bedside table. Her message read: "I never thought I would sleep in an oriental bed but now I'm convinced that cross-fertilising cultures through love is a great idea. Thank you, Said."

31

On one of those short autumn days a white envelope arrived in the mail from Oslo's municipal education department. I opened it up to find a certificate confirming I had passed the advanced Norwegian language exam and was now qualified to work and study. Language is the first gateway to discovering and adjusting to a new home country. I didn't tell Tona about my certificate but I did translate an extract from al-Sayyab's Rain Song. As soon as I'd finished, I wrote it out on coloured paper and sent it to her with the certificate:

Your eyes are two palm groves in the early light,
Or two balconies from which the moon recedes.
When your eyes smile, the grapevines come into leaf
And lights dance ... like moons in a river
Ruffled gently by an oar in the early light
Rain ... rain ... rain.

Tona memorised the poem and would repeat it whenever we ran into a shower of rain – "rain ... rain ... rain". We met every evening at the Cafe Sør in Torggata, drinking beer and chatting, then listened to live music before parting on the metro platform. We would spend Saturday and Sunday nights cross-fertilising civilisations in my flat. We had done to civilisations things that the Mongols never did to Baghdad and we shared enough happiness to make a thousand elephants fly. She suggested that since I'd passed the language exam I should register with the government employment office in case they had a job for me. Many of the people I knew had found work through this office. Although I longed to study literature, I preferred to take her advice because I needed the money, so I registered as someone seeking a civil service position. After a long wait, Mrs Isabel Lundemo, one of the staff in the office, called me in the winter of that year to tell me that the Norwegian postal service was planning to organise a training course for postal workers and she wanted to recommend me. I agreed immediately and on the morning of the next Monday we met at the employment office.

It was a very cold winter's day and it was snowing heavily non-stop, but she insisted on walking to the post office on the grounds that it was close by. She was wearing a yellow coat that reached well below her knees and hobnail boots so that she wouldn't slip on the ice. Soaked through, I walked behind her like an orphan selling Kleenex on a wintry pavement, indifferent to the snowflakes. Twenty minutes later we reached the post office. It was a tall building in the city centre, so tall and stylish that it looked like a five-star hotel.

"I've been waiting for you since ten o'clock," said Henrik Finstad, with a hint of reproach.

"That's not my fault, Mr Finstad," said Ms Lundemo, rather irritably. "Ask your assistant. Maybe she made a mistake, because our appointment was for half past ten."

"Okay, okay. I apologise, madam, please have a seat."

"No matter."

"What would you like to drink?"

"Coffee," said Isabel.

"And you?"

"A beer," I said, trying to lighten up the atmosphere, but Isabel glared at me disapprovingly, so I immediately corrected myself. "Coffee," I said, "if you please."

I learned from the session that our host, Henrik Finstad, who worked in the sorting department in the Norwegian postal service, would supervise the training and that he was the only man in a department that employed dozens of women. He seemed to be conciliatory and cautious in the way he dealt with the opposite sex. After Isabel had gone, he whispered to me, "Don't be surprised at the power of women here, Said. You're in a country where women make up a majority of the population."

"But, Mr Finstad, shouldn't that imbalance mean that we males are pampered?" I said, trying to be clever.

"No, that's not how it is. We're in the minority and minorities are usually oppressed."

"Bad luck for minorities. I thought things were different here."

Henrik rubbed the tip of his nose with his index finger and said, "Not exactly. Anyway, leave that aside for now and follow me so we can start work."

As I wandered around the post office with Henrik I realised that the reason for the power of women wasn't their numbers, but because in the post office, for example, they worked with the energy of males and the patience of females, and that made them stronger.

Anyway, all I could do was make sure I passed the test and got the job. I needed money for my mother because a malignant cancer had spread to her womb. I had to give up my dreams and do any job I could to cover her medical bills. I promised to attend the training course and Henrik became a friend to me despite the age gap between us. He was tall and very thin and looked rather pathetic, but although he was over sixty, he was still energetic at work. He had spent part of his life teaching maths in a primary school, but then he looked for another job. Changing jobs is common in Norway – it's not unusual to hear of a doctor giving up medicine, studying law and becoming a lawyer, for example, or a physics teacher becoming a nurse after getting a university degree in nursing. Henrik finally found his way to the postal service and got a job in the sorting office.

We used to smoke together during our breaks. Henrik would sometimes pour out his heart to me. He often complained about his wife, and although I don't respect men who complain about their wives to strangers, I was eager to listen to him, because listening leads to respect and affection. I never suggested any solutions or gave him any advice. How could I? But it made him happy that I listened to him. I later discovered that there wasn't any serious problem between him and his wife. There was just a breakdown in communication between them and if he had tried to fix it early he wouldn't have needed to complain. Not listening tends to weaken the bonds of love and makes homes feel more like hotels, with the guests living under the same roof but not sharing their lives with each other.

Henrik finally gave me a certificate to show I had successfully completed my training, with his signature and a stamp from the Norwegian postal service. Now that I had passed the test, I was qualified to deliver the mail. I contacted Isabel Lundemo in the employment office and told her my news. She said that meant I would soon get a job and I just had to wait. In the afternoon I called my mother and asked her to pray for me to get the job. My mother often prayed for me but she didn't always stick to what I asked her to pray for. In the past I had asked her to pray for me to be granted asylum in Norway but what she prayed was: "Oh God Almighty, grant Said success and bring him safely home." So then I said, "Hey, Mum, that's wrong. That prayer would take me back to Iraq. Pray for me to be granted asylum, not to be deported, please." And she would reply with complete confidence and indifference, "Don't worry. God can sort it out Himself. What do you know about the ways of God?"

This time I insisted that, despite her illness and the troubled frame of mind she was in these days, she should pray for the right thing: a job in the postal service, and nothing else. She promised me she would do so. One day, as I was sitting on the sofa reading the newspaper, Isabel Lundemo called me to say I'd been offered a job in the post office in Rodeløkka north of Oslo. I thanked her for her help and called my mother immediately.

"Mum, congratulate me, I've got the job," I said.

"Thank God, congratulations, my son."

"Now swear on my father's soul to tell me the truth, mum, what did you say in your prayer?"

"I said, 'Oh God Almighty, protect Said and bring him safely home.'"

I put down the phone and collapsed on the floor laughing. It was clear that the god my mother was addressing knew exactly what she wanted him to do. I told Tona the story and she laughed heartily, then crossed herself and prayed for my mother's recovery.

The next day I gathered my papers and took the bus to the post office to take on my new job.

32

One day I told Tona I'd be waiting for her at the café at eight o'clock in the evening. I arrived two hours early. I was agitated, and I kept looking at my watch and checking the door. The clock struck eight and Tona arrived. I pulled out a chair for her and stood solemnly in front of her, like one of those obsequious waiters in five-star restaurants. She laughed and her lovely eyes sparkled, and then she asked me what was behind this unusual performance. I didn't answer. I bowed, pressed the palms of my hands together as if praying, and said, "Are you willing?" She smiled, pouted then half-opened her mouth in a sign of incomprehension. Then I went down on my knees, took a ring out of my jacket pocket and presented it to her, saying, "Tona, will you marry me?" "Ah, now I understand," she said, with a laugh and a happy tear. "Yes, I will."

We later filled out the marriage papers and Tona asked me if her family name could be the name of our new family, and I agreed to her request, so from then on we were Mr and Mrs Jensen. I had never cared about family names, and I saw no difference between Mardan and Jensen, as long as I was happy. The next day I changed the name on my driving licence, my passport and my bank cards to Said Jensen. We decided to have the wedding in seven months' time to give ourselves time to buy and furnish a suitable house together. Outside work hours we were inseparable by day and we were drunk with happiness. After mastering the language and starting to swallow my words as Norwegians do, I started writing funny short stories in Norwegian. Tona edited and corrected them before we sent them for publication in the newspaper *Dagposten* in return for a modest fee that I could add to the money I earned from my job with the post office.

With Tona I discovered what life tastes like when it is mixed with joy, and I almost forgot all the disappointments, losses and defeats I had seen in life. But one day my phone rang, God damn it, and that phone call would burst the bubble of my happiness and reduce it to nothing. It was Tona who was calling.

"Hi, Said," she said.

"Hi, Honeysip," I answered as usual.

But this time she didn't laugh. "Where are you?" she said, in a voice that sounded as if she had a blocked nose.

"In the library, what's up, Tona? You sound strange."

"Nothing, I'm waiting for you in the café."

"Okay, fifteen minutes and I'll be with you."

Exactly fifteen minutes later, I walked into the Cafe Sør and saw Tona with her back to the front window, trying to hide the sadness in her eyes. Her eyelids were drooping, holding back tears that would have flooded the Hemsedal valley if she had let them flow. Her hands pressed together, she started speaking: "I want you to know, Said, that you have enriched my life and helped me grow, and if it weren't for you it would have remained as dry as a dead fig tree, with just work and reading as my daily routine. But even so, I can't continue."

I opened my mouth and my eyes like a boy who's just heard his parents have died in a car accident. Then I stared at her in the hope she would suddenly change tack and say she was joking, but she closed her eyes and shook her head in a sign that she was serious. I peppered her with all the questions swarming like bees in my head, but she dismissed them all. "Please, Said, don't make it difficult for me," she interrupted. "I know what you want to say, and you have a right to know, but it's more than I can bear. I can't, believe me." Then she took off the ring, pushed it towards me and let out all the tears she'd been holding back. I had a feeling at the time that my long experience with being shocked wouldn't save me this time. My heart was pounding in turmoil. Tona Jensen wasn't a passing moment that could easily be forgotten. She wasn't a travelling companion who might get off at the next station and disappear without a trace. She was the eye through which I saw the gentle aspect of this world. But now she was crying bitterly, with tears rolling down her cheeks like autumn rain. I pretended to get a grip, out of pity for her, holding my tongue and ignoring my own anguish. I held her hands and begged for an explanation with which I might allay my forebodings. She pulled her hands back, pressed them together and rested her bowed head on them. I took a deep breath and gave a long sigh, then I remembered how in childhood we used to make jokes to reduce the effect of shocks. "But what will happen to civilisations without you, Tona?" I said. "Who will I cross-fertilise them with on cold Saturday nights?" But she didn't laugh, and I knew the story was over and there was no going back on her decision. I took my ring and walked off, hiding my tears.

Helena Jorstad, the *Dagposten* editor who checked my short stories before they were published in the newspaper, told me later that Tona had done what she did for my sake.

"For my sake, you say?"

"Yes, she did it for your sake, Said."

"How so?"

"Tona had a kidney tumour, and her chances of recovery were very slim."

"For God's sake, what are you saying, Helena?"

"It's the truth, believe me. The doctor told her that morning."

I took out my phone and called Tona, but her number didn't seem to be in service.

"Where did you hear this?"

"Sara, the editor in the news department, told me."

"Yes, Sara was a close friend of Tona's."

I tried calling Tona again, but without success. The

number was clearly out of service.

"Where is she now? I haven't seen her in the city for ages."

"She stopped working at the school and left the city."

"For where?"

"She went back to her mother's house in Bergen."

"My god. Tona loved me so much she thought it would ruin my life if she stayed around as she counted the days she had left to live, so on the basis of a mere assumption she threw away everything we shared and left!"

Her number was still not working.

I rushed to the news department at the newspaper and asked Sara for Tona's address in Bergen, but she refused to give it to me. She asked me to respect Tona's wish that no one should know the address. I then called the post office and told them I couldn't come to work for the rest of the week. I went home, stuffed a small shoulder bag with a few clothes and headed to the train station the next morning. I had decided to go to Bergen to find Tona and bring her back, because life is made to be shared with all its opposites: happiness and sadness, health and illness, wealth and poverty. If it wasn't like that, it wouldn't be worth living.

If only Tona had told me, I swear I would have given her one of my kidneys and we could have continued our journey through life together. But alas, she didn't. She got off at the first station and left me alone to face my own ordeal. I stood by the ticket machine in Oslo's main railway station, tapped in the letters of the word Bergen in the destination box and went through all the steps till the PAY prompt appeared on the screen. I took my bank card out of my wallet and inserted it in the machine, tapped in the pin number and took my Oslo-Bergen ticket. As I went to platform 3, my phone began to ring and it was Helena Jorstad calling.

"Ms Jorstad, what can I do for you?

"My sympathies for you, my friend," she said.

"Why? What's happened?"

"Tona's died. Her mother just called and told Sara the news."

I broke down completely. I collapsed by the ticket machine with excruciating pains in my head, and was taken to hospital. This would be the first time I had met Dr Stefan Holmberg, but it wouldn't be the last.

33

Without Tona I grew more isolated and my day was divided between two activities – a job that I couldn't stand but that provided me with an income to meet my needs, and my writing, which I loved and to which I devoted many hours for meagre payment. One took place by day and the other by night. These two were all I had in this icy life of mine. After finishing my postal round at four p.m. I went home exhausted, changed my clothes, silenced my stomach with whatever food was available, and then had an hour's nap that would inevitably be troubled by nightmares. When I woke up, I would withdraw to my study to write stories for a regular column on the back page of the *Dagposten*. As time passed, Helena gave me special treatment and would wait till late at night while I put the finishing touches on a story to amuse her newspaper readers. She would edit it and then send it straight to the printing press.

It was my job to make the readers laugh and raise the level of adrenaline in their blood, but it was hard to do this when I was in such low spirits after Tona's death. I often increased the dose of ketamine I took when things got me down, and then I would imagine my study full of pink-faced men and women who would start laughing. I would stand in front of them like a comedian on a small stage and proceed to tell them jokes, some innocent and others rather darker. These jokes would form the basis for the stories I would write. The place would ring with laughter and shouts and clapping. The show would pick up pace until I finally dealt them the punchline and had them in tears. And while they were clapping and laughing, I would sneak away behind the screen to write down the story, then send it to Helena accompanied by a dirty joke. The effects of the ketamine would gradually wear off, and the audience would depart, leaving me to drink the cup of my loneliness. In the morning I would read the newspaper before going to work and say to myself, "What a happy man he must be, the man who wrote that story!"

34

Smoke filled the hallway and my mother ran out of the kitchen with her dress in flames. She had left the gas on and fallen asleep. When she woke up to the smell, the gas bottle exploded. She tried to put out the fire but it was no use. The flames had destroyed half the house, reducing it to ashes. A gallant neighbour jumped into the fire to save her, took her out of the rising flames, but then she gave him the slip and went back inside. She had remembered that I was still asleep in the room. The man tried to stop her going back inside for fear the ceiling would fall in on her but he didn't succeed. She kicked the door to the room and went in. I was pointing the camera towards the door to record the moment when my mother came out carrying me in her arms. "Where's my grave?" someone whispered in my ear. I turned to him and he had covered his face with a black rag. I reached out to remove the damned piece of cloth, but then my mother came out of the fire carrying me, and the ceiling fell in on us, and the image of my father vanished.

I threw off the cover, jumped out of bed, got dressed and left for the shops. I bought an international phone card, a packet of coffee and some cigarettes. I hurried back and made a cup of coffee. I picked up the phone, scratched the foil off the phone card and tapped in Abir's number. She had given me her number once and told me only to call her if necessary. Her unexpected request that I go back to Iraq was still ringing in my head, but she still wasn't answering my messages. I was going to call her, regardless of the consequences, I told myself as I dialled. Luckily, she was alone and her call didn't catch her at an embarrassing moment. She said the Internet had been down because a stray shell had hit a communications tower and the company had been repairing it since one p.m. and it might be fixed in a few hours. She avoided talking about her last message, which had had the same effect on me as a rifle shot on a flock of pigeons. She spoke about work, her latest projects and the exhibition of photographs she was organising on the banks of the Tigris. She said that Baghdad was now a paradise and a month never went by without an art exhibition or some major cultural event. Then she started advising me not to listen to tendentious media that tried to tarnish Iraq's reputation as if they had an old grudge against Gilgamesh. "Iraq is paradise, Said, believe me," she repeated.

"Abir, cut out the crazy talk and tell me why it's so important I should come back," I interrupted.

She didn't reply. She tried to avoid the subject but, with only a few minutes left on my phone card, I insisted on a precise answer: "What is it exactly, Abir? For God's sake, tell me."

"They've found your father," she said, in an unusually sympathetic tone. "You have to come back to pick up his remains."

The balance on my phone card expired.

35

The night seemed darker than usual and the sky gloomier. I was standing on the balcony, chain-smoking until my lungs were burning from so much smoking and I started coughing so loudly the neighbours might have thought I was knocking on their door. The cigarette smoke then thickened and started to form a white cloud that covered the residential district around me. The cloud lifted a little and took on the shape of a wide-eyed ghost with a long beard that covered two thirds of its face and the top of its neck. My mother had never told me that my father was one of those men who let their beards grow long. I lit another cigarette in the hope it might add the final touch to my father's face, but the neighbourhood dog appeared under the balcony and barked twice: "Woof, woof." I came to my senses and my father vanished. The dog was saying, "You've stayed up long enough, you idiot. We want to sleep." I went inside and closed the balcony door. I went to the bedroom, possibly to have a nap before going to the post office, but there was a notification from the laptop, which I had forgotten to shut down. It was Abir on a chat app, saying that a few days earlier the agency she worked for had assigned her to cover an event that would be of interest to me. The Iraqi Red Crescent had found a mass grave near al-Kifl, south of Baghdad, and witnesses said it probably contained the remains of forty leftist opponents of the old regime, buried secretly thirty-seven years ago. They planned to open it up in the coming week.

"Did you hear how old the grave is? The authorities think it includes the remains of Nassir Mardan. You must come back at once, Said. Are you listening?" I didn't respond. My eyes filled with tears as soon as I heard the news and I could no longer see the screen in front of me. I closed the laptop and pushed it aside. I changed my clothes and at that late hour of night went out. I reached the post office three hours before my shift began. The post office was shut because the evening shift had finished work and gone home. I turned off the engine, pushed the seat back, stretched out my legs under the steering wheel, pulled my hat down over my eyes and waited.

36

After his accident Daniel was no longer a postman. His spine was damaged and he was out of work. One day I saw him coming into a shopping centre in a wheelchair. I went up to him to say hello but he didn't recognise me, or pretended he didn't.

"Daniel, I'm Said. Have you forgotten me?" I said.

"Do I even know you, to forget you? What did you say your name was?"

"Said, your colleague at the post office."

"Said! Is that a person's name or a door squeaking? Get out of my face, you idiot."

Daniel certainly seemed strange and abnormally aggressive. I walked off, putting his behaviour down to events and their effect on people's characters. After all, we humans are as weak as flies that have had their wings pulled off. But he called me back: "Just a moment please, if you will."

"What's up?" I asked.

"Have you ever seen a five-legged frog?"

"No, I haven't."

"Neither have I!" he replied, then burst into laughter in the same old way. He opened his arms to me and I gave him a hug. Then I knelt down and we started reminiscing about the days when we delivered the mail together. When I reminded him of some incidents he would purse his lips, close his eyes and slap the palm of his hand on his forehead. I felt there was a sadness deep inside him and he was trying to hold back tears. I massaged his shoulders and reminded him of what he had once said about life being a short film and how, if some disaster strikes, you should just repeat to yourself the words "Short film, short film, short film", and then the disaster would melt away like snow in the sun. He patted my hand and said, "That's right." Then he invited me to a pizza in a fancy restaurant nearby. We sat down, chatted and laughed a lot, then I said goodbye and left. The next day I saw my boss, Kari Solberg, in the street. That put me in a bad mood and even made me want to vomit. She had an extraordinary ability to irritate people and make them feel depressed. I followed Daniel's advice and chanted to myself "Short film, short film, short film." But she didn't melt away like ice or disappear.

37

The staff started to turn up. I was watching the building through half-closed eyes. Kari Solberg finally arrived, wearing a grey summer jacket and looking out over glasses perched on the end of her nose. She saw me lying in the van, with both my feet resting on the steering wheel. She shook her head in a deliberate gesture of disapproval, then walked on. I waited till she went inside, then took my feet down and pulled the seat upright. I straightened up my clothing and went to the door of her office. I knocked but she didn't answer. She was inside, I knew that, but she didn't want to see me. I opened the door anyway and she reacted angrily.

"I didn't give you permission to come in."

"*Tuzz*," I swore in Arabic.

"Speak Norwegian please. And why aren't you wearing your work clothes? Did anyone tell you the post van is meant for sleeping in rather than work?"

I didn't care about her nonsense. I put my resignation letter on her desk and turned to go.

"Wait, let me see," she shouted, picking up my letter and starting to read in a low voice. Her annoyance soon turned to delight. Hiding a smile, she picked up a pen and signed her approval. Then she told me she would tell the accounts department to complete the paper work. I left her office without saying goodbye, slammed the door behind me. I slammed the door shut behind me with such force that I felt her excellency the manager would leap up and her head hit the ceiling. I walked to the end of the corridor, then turned into the personnel department office. I handed in a bag of work clothes, the keys to the van and some important documents that had been in my care. Then I left the post office, never to return. I took the 31 bus to the city centre. Through the window I could see it was raining. People were carrying umbrellas and calmly going about the business of living. Oslo seemed unfamiliar that day, though I knew the city by heart and could walk the streets with my eyes closed. The bus finally stopped. I got out and hurried across the street to a small shop. I bought an umbrella, then turned into Stenersgata Street and went into the Oslo City shopping centre. I bought a suitcase and some clothes, then went to a shop on the third floor that sold photographic equipment. I bought a charger for my camera and a memory stick, then went back to the bus station.

Working for the post office hadn't left me much time for photography, but I had taken quite a number of pictures over the years. I had taken some of Tona, who had died too early and had made my life as lonely as an abandoned grave, and also of Daniel, Mercedes, my neighbour with the long white hair, and other people I had loved in this cold country.

I went back home, picked up my laptop and started searching for an early flight to Baghdad. I couldn't find any in the next ten days. That meant I wouldn't be in time for the opening of the grave. I looked for flights to Amman, but the earlier the date, the more expensive the tickets. In the end I had to buy an expensive one but at least it was leaving the next day. I packed my suitcase with clothes, the camera and some papers, then took the wooden frame off the wall in the study and stuffed it into my luggage. The frame would finally hold a picture of my father. I shut the suitcase and parked it by the door, then placed my passport and my wallet on top. I went to the kitchen, took two slices of bread out of the fridge, toasted them, put a slice of cheese between them, and started to munch the sandwich standing. After that I made a cup of coffee and went back to sitting at the computer. I opened Yahoo Messenger to contact Abir, only to find a barrage of messages she had left me – messages full of reproach, fear, apprehension and anxiety. She was worried something unfortunate had happened to me since she had told me about the mass grave.

I was sure my father had died. With a stroke of a pen, some functionary had ordered him executed and now he was just a shadowy memory. But I had never considered the possibility that I might be invited to collect his remains from a mass grave. I wrote an apology to Abir because I hadn't replied the previous day. I was about to log off when Abir appeared online. She bombarded me with more words of reproach for the unjustified anxiety I had caused her. Anxiety is one of the signs that someone is in love, so this girl seemed to be in love with me despite the distance between us. God damn distances. To calm her down, I sent her an invitation to switch into video mode. She accepted, and popped up on my screen like an angel. But the sound, alas, was patchy.

"Your voice is breaking up, Abir," I wrote. "Rest assured, I'm fine and I apologise for my bad behaviour yesterday, but the news was hard to take."

"Never mind, my dear. Anyway, what do you plan to do?"

She had a power cut and the back-up power supply started to make a whistling noise.

"Oh god, there's a power cut, Said. Tell me quickly, please, before the back-up cuts off and the computer closes down. What do you plan to do?"

"I'm coming back tomorrow."

She read my message and disappeared from the screen.

38

The driver ignored the red light at the end of the road. He just shot across the junction brazenly and drove on at speed. Soon I heard the police car behind us. Someone must have called and reported the man's driving. Sitting in the back seat, I asked him to slow down, since we still had plenty of time before our departure. He didn't react. He turned right without touching the brakes. He started driving at a crazy speed. I grabbed his shirt collar and shook him but he didn't notice. I looked at his face in the rear-view mirror and the flesh on his face had started to melt. It was my father. At the top of my voice, I shouted at him to turn around so that I could know what he looked like before he disappeared. He let go of the steering wheel and turned around for me to see him, but then the car tipped over and my father disappeared.

When I came to my senses, the traffic light had turned green and the car was slowly turning towards the entrance to Oslo's international airport. I paid the driver, took out my suitcase and walked away.

39

"Last call for Turkish Airlines flight 319, bound for Amman via Istanbul. Would passengers please proceed to boarding gate D23," the announcer called three times over the PA system.

I finished my cup of coffee and put my laptop in my backpack, then headed to gate D23. I slipped my boarding pass into my passport and stood in the queue. With an affected smile, the airline woman stamped our passes and gave them back to us. I identified my seat on the plane, turned off my mobile phone and put it in my backpack. I put the backpack in the overhead locker, sat and watched the pretty stewardess explaining the safety instructions in sign language. The plane finally took off and then levelled off for the long cruise. Through the window I took a farewell look at Norway below me. Sunbeams lit up mountain peaks covered in green and surrounded by blue fjords. It looked like a picture postcard. Farewell to the land of water and mountains.

40

"Welcome," I said.

"Hmmph," he said grumpily.

He was as bad-tempered as a mountain goat, but his face soon changed and he smiled when I showed him my red passport with the Norwegian coat of arms. He stamped it immediately with an entry permit for Jordan and said "Welcome" properly this time.

"There you are, sir, at your service," he added.

"Thank you."

Those red European passports with their national crests have achieved something that the Arab League has failed to do in all the years since it was founded. This kind of passport turns an Arab traveller into a respected person at Arab airports and at the same time frees you from all the ethnic considerations that once marked you out from other Arabic speakers. Despite all the bombastic nationalist slogans that you were taught at school in "national education" classes, and that you would come across, when you grew up, on posters at border posts, a red passport has become the only way to join a club whose members enjoy respect and esteem. Shocking but true.

I picked up my luggage and took a taxi that was standing near the airport entrance. I was impatient to see my friend Salam and taste the falafel he made. The driver was listening to a sermon on the radio. "Downtown, please," I told him.

"If God on high wishes," he replied, with inexplicable piety.

By the time we reached downtown the sound of the radio had turned my head into a drum. I paid the zealot driver, took my suitcase and crossed the main road. I took the third street on the right and walked towards Salam's old restaurant. But I couldn't find it. At first, I thought I was lost and would have to go back to where the taxi dropped me off. But when I asked a passer-by, he pointed to a money-changer's shop and said, "Salam the Iraqi's restaurant used to be here."

"And where can I find Salam, please?" I asked the man at the desk inside, who was also Iraqi.

"You mean Salam al-Iraqi?"

"Exactly."

"I tell you, Salam left the country long ago," the man replied.

"Where to?" I asked.

"Australia. He sold the restaurant and went there. Please, have a seat."

"No, thanks."

So Salam had emigrated. He had gone to Australia in search of a "full-fat" rest. I don't think you'll find it, my friend. Alternative countries do not give us complete rest, when we have already spent a third of our lives in a place where there are narrow lanes, houses packed side by side, and the smell of bread from clay ovens. However benevolent and peace-loving those new countries might be, we long for the street in which we first played football with our friends. I remember once winning a football match for barefooted players, and my team was given a cup and some medals. At the time the cup was made of cardboard and the medals of Pepsi Cola bottle tops, with a hole drilled through them and a cotton thread for a chain. I have no idea what fate befell that precious cup, but I still have the medal, which I count as the most precious prize I have ever won.

I said goodbye to the money-changer and went into a small restaurant nearby. I was yearning for falafel. I hadn't had any since leaving Amman many years ago. I paid the bill and went off with my bag in search of a cheap hotel, the kind of hotel where I could see crowds from the balcony, a hotel planted in the heart of the city, in an area no doubt teeming with people. I missed the sight of crowded streets. In Norway you never see a street full of people. There are only a few million people in the whole country, whereas four million people live in the city of Amman, a tract of land about twenty-five miles across.

That night I went to sleep to the sound of people. In the morning I went to a travel office and booked a ticket to Baghdad. The clerk said trips to Baghdad started at dawn and there were two kinds of vehicles – air-conditioned buses or large SUVs, which could take eight passengers and were also air-conditioned. I booked the two front seats in one of the SUVs so that I could sit more comfortably. I spent the day wandering around the shops and cafés, then went back to the hotel. I packed my bag, which was almost ready. I looked at the frame for my father's picture. "Frames were made for pictures of human beings, not for piles of bones, silly," the frame whispered to me. I stuffed it into the bag and closed it, and at 4 a.m. I was ready and waiting in front of the travel office.

41

It was July 7, approaching midday. The sun was melting the tarmac and the highway to Baghdad was almost deserted. For hours I had seen only a few cars, with families, driving the other way towards Jordan. I asked Wa'il, the talkative driver of the GMC vehicle, why people were leaving the country and heading for Jordan. "God alone knows," he replied. Then he starting chatting about politics, economics, sport and the price of cars.

I couldn't understand how leaving home could be such an easy choice. Two whole years had passed without war. Wasn't that enough to persuade people to stay? I wanted to turn back so I could share my thoughts with them and find out why they were leaving. There must be another explanation, unknown to those living abroad like me, because putting your hand in water is not like putting your hand in fire, as the proverb goes.

The driver threw out a cigarette end and closed the window to put the air-conditioning back on. He hadn't stopped talking since he started the engine. First, he gave out cards with his name and phone number, repeating the words: "Wa'il GMC. Ask for me and you'll find me." He gave us just too much information about himself. He said he had graduated from the college of engineering at Baghdad University but couldn't find a job, so he'd decided to work as a driver on the Amman route. But he didn't have enough money to do that, so he had to ask his rich uncle to buy the vehicle in return for half of the proceeds.

"My uncle sleeps on a green bed," he said.
"A green bed! What do you mean?" I asked in surprise.
"I mean a bed of dollars, sir."
"Aha, and are you happy working on the GMC?"
"Can't complain, sir."
"Wa'il, for God's sake, don't call me sir," I said.
"Okay, sir," he said with a smile, and we laughed.

He went from speaking about his uncle to speaking about politics, America and the political parties. Then he switched, I don't know how, to football and al-Jawiya Club, which ran in his veins like blood, he said. Then he took out a bundle of Indian joss-sticks and stuck one in front of the air conditioning vent. It gave off a pungent, soporific smoke that made one's eyelids droop. The driver turned up the radio and started to hum along to a George Wassouf song: "*Love is king, love is king / O lovers, love is king.*" I begged him to turn it down and sank into my seat in hope of a short nap. But something went wrong with the engine and we ground to a halt. I couldn't imagine how this new GMC could suddenly break down. Wa'il slammed his fist down on the steering wheel and cursed the day he started working as a driver. After a string of curses, he got out, opened the engine cover to find out where the problem lay. "Son of a bitch," he shouted after inspecting the engine.

"What's the problem, Wa'il?" I asked.

"Disaster, sir. There's not a drop of petrol in it," he said.

"So where did all the petrol go? Didn't you fill it up before we left?" I asked.

"No. The gauge said it was full, but it doesn't seem to be working."

So there we were, out of petrol, and there wasn't a filling station anywhere near. Wa'il tried to call his office on his mobile phone but the mobile network hadn't reached that area yet.

"Well, what do we do now?" one of the passengers asked.

"I don't know," said Wa'il.

"And you're the one who should know," said the passenger.

Then the two men started quarrelling and would have

hit each other if we hadn't kept them apart. Iraqi blood soon comes to the boil, especially in the summer.

I sat by the side of the road, took out a packet of cigarettes and lit one. I offered it to the hapless driver and then lit one for myself, so that we could blow smoke into the air together. How would we get out of this mess? Baghdad was still a long way off, across the desert that stretched beyond the horizon, and there were so few petrol stations along the highway that the closest one was probably twenty miles away. My god, what bad luck! The passengers started to grumble and got into futile arguments with the driver. Wa'il tried calling his office again and again, but to no avail. There was no network. Our ordeal lasted two hours, two hours scorched by the blazing sun and bathed in sweat. We were waiting for a vehicle, any vehicle that might give us a few litres of petrol, enough to get us to the nearest petrol station, but nothing came. In the end a convoy of vehicles came into sight in the distance. They were military tracked and armoured vehicles, flying the Stars and Stripes. Each vehicle had a white metal board with a message in English and in Arabic, warning people not to approach. We waved them down for help. A Humvee stopped and troops primed to pull their triggers got out of the vehicle. They told us to move back and put our hands in the air like POWs. They were frightened and wary. As if we were the killers and they were the victims! They searched us thoroughly, every inch of our bodies, so much so that we thought they must be inspecting us for piles rather than for guns. Once they had established that we didn't have any weapons, they asked why we had stopped. When we explained the problem, one of the Americans took a jerrycan of petrol off the back of the Humvee, a jerrycan with a picture of a green ghoul on the side. I had never seen such a picture before and I had never heard of a petrol can having such a picture. Anyway, the driver emptied the petrol into the fuel tank and the engine started.

The GMC set off singing towards Baghdad, but this clearly wasn't regular fuel. The SUV was driving like a blind rocket. I asked Wa'il to slow down. He couldn't. He swore on his mother's honour that he couldn't slow down and had lost control of the brakes. He was holding the steering wheel tight in an attempt to tame the vehicle. But it raced on and the road dissolved into a streaking blur. After that, Wa'il gave up trying to control it and kept himself busy by shrieking like a woman. The others started shrieking too, while I found the scene so strange that I was tongue-tied in amazement, and silent as a stone by the roadside. I was alarmed at what was happening and frightened I might meet my demise on the outskirts of Baghdad before I even saw the city again. My god, have I come all this way to die in a bizarre road accident? The GMC pursued its manic dash until I thought it would explode and our body parts would be scattered in the air. But finally the vehicle settled down. I opened my eyes and saw a large sign: "Welcome to Baghdad".

42

Trees pruned to exactly the same height stood like palace guards along both sides of a long paved road leading to a high gateway made of bricks and marble. There were towering suspension bridges across the Tigris that looked like swings in the sky. White boats lined the river banks. I stuck my head out of the car window and breathed in the smell of Baghdad. It made my head spin, like a wine two hundred years old or more. My ears picked up sad *maqam* music, but it made me feel as happy as a lover who has smelt the neck of his beloved. I remembered what Abir had said about Baghdad now being paradise, and I regretted I hadn't believed her at the time. I did have my doubts – no sensible person would believe that a city on which thousands of tonnes of bombs had fallen could still be standing on its own two feet, let alone believe the city was now paradise. "What's really going on, Baghdad?" I wondered. "There we are, guys, safely arrived," said the driver, interrupting my thoughts. He said we were at the Allawi station, a large well-maintained garage with modern buses lined up along the sides, bound for other Iraqi cities. At the gate stood a small device with a green button and underneath it said, "Call a taxi." I pressed the button and a message appeared on a screen: "Thank you. Your request will be answered immediately." Three minutes later a black Mercedes arrived with an illuminated taxi sign on top. A young man got out wearing black trousers and a white shirt with his company's logo on it. He picked up my bag, put it in the boot and said, "Please." I opened the front door and sat next to him.

"Where would you like to go, sir?" he asked me politely.

"New Baghdad, please."

"Any particular place in New Baghdad?"

"Behind the Syriac quarter, close to Hamza the herbalist's shop."

I had the impression he was annoyed by my answer. "Sir, please give me a detailed address so that I can put it in the GPS," he said.

"Sorry, I don't have many details. I left Iraq many years ago and all I remember is that my aunt's house is there."

"So?"

"So, let's play it by ear. You take me to New Baghdad and I'll handle it from there."

"Okay, right you are."

I had to see Jalal there, because I missed him badly. As soon as we set off, the polite driver turned the radio to Radio Dar al-Salam. A local news bulletin began, read by a female announcer who pronounced her Arabic very correctly. The first piece of news was that the Baghdad Municipality was planning to sign a contract with a

German railway company to build an underground train network in Baghdad. The next piece was that the tenth tranche of apartments for people with special needs would be assigned the coming Tuesday. The third item was light news: a doctor had caught a rat in the storerooms of a government hospital and had taken a souvenir picture of herself and the rat, to mark the first visit to the hospital by a rat.

"What do you think of Baghdad after all these years, sir?" asked the driver, after turning the radio down.

"Paradise," I said, looking out of the window at a skyscraper hotel.

The news bulletin ended and a programme of Iraqi songs followed. I asked the driver to turn the radio up a little so that we could hear. He did, but I wished he hadn't, for it was Saadoun Jabir singing a tear-jerker religious song: "O mother, O mother of faith, O blessing from heaven, O tent of goodness and faith, you have brought us all together through love." I really did shed a tear at this, which I wouldn't have done if my mother had been waiting for me at the door. We reached New Baghdad without me noticing the time, because the roads weren't crowded despite the thousands of vehicles about. The municipality had got rid of the junctions that led to bottlenecks and replaced them with flyovers and tunnels. Not only that, but the driver told me he had read in the newspaper that in four years' time Baghdad was going to declare itself a city free of traffic lights.

"Congratulations, bro. Even Oslo doesn't have town

planning of that quality," I said.

"Oslo Shmoslo. This is Baghdad, sir," he replied.

"Indeed, it is Baghdad. Okay, drop me here, please. I've arrived."

"With pleasure."

As soon as my feet touched the ground, I felt very confused and puzzled. New Baghdad had greatly changed and the old landmarks had disappeared. The streets were still wide and the pavements tidy. The gardens were full of eucalyptus trees with flocks of happy little birds on their branches. I walked around aimlessly, too shy to ask for a pathetic herbalist's shop. But as I was walking across a park, I caught sight of a dignified man in a grey suit, sitting on a bench. An old woman, dressed in black, her hair covered with a small brown scarf, was leaning on his shoulder. I picked up my bag and headed towards them. I greeted them and asked them where I might find Hamza the herbalist's shop. The old woman said they were new to the area and didn't know anyone by that name. I thanked her and was about to walk on when she grabbed my hand and asked me to sit down. I sat down. The woman put her hand in a bag close by and took out a carton of juice and a chocolate bar. "Here you are, son, this is Duraid's reward," she said mysteriously. Her white hand trembled like a leaf, while the old man bowed his head in sadness. I stayed with them, chewing slowly on the chocolate bar and listening to the sad old woman. They said they had lost their only son, Duraid, in an American air raid on

Baghdad in 2003. He was working at the time as an engineer in the Allawiya telephone exchange, which was left as a pile of junk after the raid. After his death they thought their house was full of ghosts, which disturbed their sleep, so they decided to move. They sold the house in Aadhamiya and came to a small flat in one of the tower blocks in New Baghdad. The bereft mother said they spent the day in the park and nobody bothered them or asked where they had moved from, or what religion or sect they belonged to. Then she gave a long sigh. "Oh, my son, death doesn't ask about religion or sect. Go and ask Duraid, if you don't believe me."

I kissed her forehead and left the park. On the right side of the road I noticed a small kiosk that sold mobile phone accessories. I rushed towards it, like a boy who's found his mother, and bought a telephone SIM card and a top-up card. I took out the Telenor SIM card from Norway and threw it in the bin. Then I put the Iraqi card in its place, put back the battery and the cover and pressed the green key. I copied the numbers stored on the phone onto the SIM card and called Abir. "Sorry, the number you have called may be switched off or beyond network coverage. Please try again later," the recorded message said.

43

I used to call my mother regularly and she would pass on news of Jalal, the only bright spot in the story of Papa Aflaq. She told me he had married and had a beautiful daughter called Hala. She said it was her grandmother who gave her that name, after the daughter of Saddam Hussein, whose pictures were all over the walls of the house. After getting married, Jalal opened a barber's shop in our area and he would come by to look in on my mother every evening after closing time. He would go with her when she had chemotherapy and he made sure she never missed a session. I knew he would do that but what really surprised me was how obstinately my mother insisted on staying at home till the last day in her life.

One very cold night in Norway I remembered that I didn't have any international phone cards, so I decided to go out to get one. I put on my coat and a hat thick enough to keep a cow warm, then protected my feet with fur-lined boots and went down to the car park. I found the cars were buried in snow and looked like small white hillocks. I hate open-air car parks. I picked up a shovel and started removing the snow from the back of the car. After that I scraped off the viciously tenacious ice that had formed on the windows, and sat down at the wheel. I turned the key but the engine didn't respond. I tried again many times, but to no avail. The engine had sworn it wouldn't start till cocks laid eggs. And since on that icy night I couldn't find a cock I could persuade to lay eggs, I decided to make the journey on foot. It wasn't far to the grocery, but walking on ice slows you down and makes it seem much further. You also have to be very careful not to slip and fall. In Norway I had discovered the smug satisfaction of surviving a winter without bruises or fractures. I finally reached the shop, bought a phone card that would last two hours, two packets of cigarettes, and the cheese triangles that Kaka Sirvan the shopkeeper always had in stock, and a small loaf of bread. I went back to the flat, shook the snowflakes off my shoulders at the door, stamped my feet on the floor twice to clear my boots of snow and went inside. I took off the coat, hat and boots and went to the kitchen, made a quick cup of tea, and took some bread from the packet. I put it in the oven to heat up. After taking it out, I spread two pieces of cheese on it and sprinkled some Syrian zaatar on top, then rolled it up into a zaatar and cheese sandwich. I sat in the sitting room in front of the television having dinner. As I chewed on the sandwich, I tapped the card number into the phone and dialled our house in Baghdad.

By this time my mother's condition had grown serious and I would call every night to check up on her. She would say she was well and that the medicine she had recently starting taking was very helpful. But I didn't believe what she said. The pain in her voice and her breathlessness told a completely different story. The telephone rang but no one picked up. I called again and no one picked up. At that point the piece of sandwich in my mouth stopped moving, and my mind began to teem with anxious thoughts. I stood up and went to the balcony, then called again ten times, to no avail. I was sure my mother had passed away. A deep sadness started to dig its claws into my heart. I threw the phone to the floor and shouted to high heaven: "Why all this, Lord? What have I done to you? Tell me?" But someone rang the doorbell, bringing an end to the torrent of reproaches that had started to flow. I wiped my tears away with the sleeve of my shirt and opened the door. For some reason the hallway was dark but there was someone standing in front of me. I didn't recognise him. He was tall and thin, with a woollen hat or maybe a hood on his head and a piece of cloth over his mouth. "Where's my grave?" he said, in a voice I recognised. I reached out to take the cloth off his mouth, but he vanished and the hallway lights came on again.

44

I didn't know what had come over Abir. I called her a thousand times but her phone was always out of network. I had given up hope of reaching Jalal but I didn't want to give up hope of hearing Abir's voice. They were all I had in Baghdad. I called the taxi company and took a taxi to Bab al-Sharqi. I decided to stay in a hotel there until I could find a way to my uncle's house, which was lost in the maze of new buildings and roads. I asked the driver to choose a good hotel for me, and he did so willingly. The Baghdad taxi drivers are so kind! He took me to a large hotel between Tahrir Square and the Jumhuriya Bridge, dropped me at the entrance and left. The receptionist gave me a choice of floors and I chose the thirteenth floor on the eastern side. I wanted the pleasure of seeing Baghdad from above. From there the view was magical. Bab al-Sharqi looks out on Tahrir Square and I saw tall buildings with brightly lit shop windows at street level and flashing adverts on massive screens above. In the middle was a giant fountain that played like one of the dancing girls in *A Thousand and One Nights*. As I looked down from on high, surprised and happy at the same time, I remembered my friend in exile, Jamal Saadoun, and I wished I could see him to apologise for making fun of him when he said Baghdad would become Las Vegas. Jamal was right. Baghdad had become that, and deservedly so. I closed the balcony door, crooning to myself, "Baghdad, the bastion of lions, ta-ra ta-ra, beacon of the ancient world, ta-ra ta-ra . . ." I had a refreshing shower, got changed and prepared to go out for a quick walk around, but suddenly I felt dizzy and fell to the floor. When I came to, I saw a woman in a white uniform standing close by.

"Where am I?" I asked.

"You're lucky to be safe. You're in hospital."

"Did you say in hospital? What happened?"

"Nothing much. Just exhaustion. Nothing more," she said.

A young doctor came after that and said I'd have to stay with them till the next day, so that they could do some lab tests. I nodded compliance and put my head on the pillow to try to sleep. The doctor left and shut the door behind him. I pulled the white sheet over my head. I can never sleep with my face exposed. But as soon as the sheet covered my face, I remembered something strange about the room. The calendar on the wall showed the wrong date. I pulled the sheet off my face and had a close look. Yes, the date was wrong. The calendar said it was July 7, 2023, but that was nonsense. It was still 2005. It must have been a printing error or a prank like the ones that have started appearing on the satellite television channels these days, I said to myself, and dived back under the sheet. Then suddenly I jumped out of bed in a panic: I remembered that a sign outside the hotel, advertising a concert, also referred to 2023. My god, what was going on? How had all those years gone by? I pressed the button above the bed, and the nurse arrived.

"Yes, sir, what can I do to help?" she asked.

"Might I know what this is?" I said, pointing to the calendar on the wall.

"A calendar," she replied.

"I know it's a calendar. Did anyone call it anything else? But what's the date on it? How come it's skipped eighteen years?"

The nurse squinted, scratched her forehead with the tip of her finger, put her hand in her pocket and took out a small thermometer to slip into my bottom.

"Get that damned thing away from me and give me an answer. Why have you messed with the date?"

"Please calm down, sir," she replied, coldly and confidently. "That date's correct, believe me."

"What do you mean the date's correct? Is it now 2023?"

"Yes, and today's Friday, July 7, 2023."

When I heard what the nurse had said I rushed to the cupboard on the wall, took off my hospital gown and put my normal clothes on. Then I asked her to bring me the bill so I could leave. She said my stay in hospital was free, paid for by the state, and she asked me to wait till the doctor in charge gave me permission to leave. But I refused outright, signed a document saying I took full responsibility for my decision, and left. At the door I called Wa'il, the GMC driver.

"Wa'il, tell me what the hell is happening. How come it's 2023?"

"What's up, sir? Haven't you heard?"

"Heard what?"

"Heard what happened with that petrol from the American soldiers."

"You mean the blue ghoul?"

"Yes, exactly."

"What's up with that bullshit?"

"That's strange. Didn't you know it made us travel through time?"

"Yeah, sure, and did we travel with or without a visa?" I replied.

"Sir, with or without a visa, it's as I explained," he answered seriously. "You seem to have forgotten how fast the GMC went that time." Then he called off.

I was speechless from shock. But I pulled myself together and went back to the hotel. I turned on my laptop and Googled the words "blue ghoul". Hundreds of links appeared on the screen, about various types of spirit, and stories about wizards and the jinn. Arabs love jinn stories and are eager to find out how things are in the United Republics of Spirits. That's why you'll find Internet search engines full of such material. I translated the term into English, added the work "fuel" and came across a long article about a invention patented by the scientific research branch of the US Department of

Defense. Registered on July 1, 1994, it involved a sophisticated vehicle fuel with an unusual ability to interact electroluminescently, which led in turn to an escape from the bonds of gravity and an acceleration of time. This invention, according to the report, was tested only in the third Gulf War in 2003.

As I read this extraordinary article, I remembered that Henrik Finstad in the post office had once told me America saw ruined countries as laboratory mice. I didn't believe him at the time. I even said he was exaggerating. But what was especially surprising was how patient America was, waiting all those years to find a ruined country in which to test its invention. I closed the laptop. "Never mind, never mind," I mumbled. "Let them test. They've already tested lots of bombs, and radioactive and carcinogenic substances on us. So what harm does it do if they try out a vehicle fuel that speeds up time? At any rate, we'll hardly have noticed the thousands of defeats we must have suffered during those eighteen years."

45

"Now the party begins," I shouted as I ended my conversation with customer service in the hotel. I had ordered a fancy dinner with a bottle of whisky and ice cubes. I had decided to drink a toast to the blue ghoul, without whom I would have had to live through eighteen years that were no doubt full of disappointments. Disappointments don't hurt us when they pass unnoticed. In that case we have to endure only the sense of disappointment, and not the disappointment itself. Disappointments are harmless under anaesthetic. The waiter brought my order. He pushed an elegant food trolley with a dark purple tablecloth into the middle of the room, and then, very politely and tastefully, asked me if I needed anything else.

"Yes," I said. "I have a question if you don't mind."

"Sure."

"For God's sake tell me how Baghdad came to be like this after everything that happened," I said. "What did you do to bring it back to life and turn it into a paradise?"

The waiter smiled and said, "No need for surprise, sir. It's been exactly twenty years since the fall and destruction of Baghdad. Even if we'd had a government of donkeys, it would have done what you see now, and more."

I felt embarrassed in the waiter's presence, because obviously, given all those years, a desert could be turned into a city with skyscrapers, and any government in the world, however ignorant or retarded or despicable it might be, could rebuild what had been destroyed in much less time than that. I slipped a ten-dollar tip into his hand and he left, closing the door behind him. I pushed the trolley towards the balcony and brought the laptop over. I opened my song files and chose one that suited a party of this kind. Umm Kulthoum started singing:

O my heart, don't ask where love is.
It towered in my imagination and collapsed.
Give me water to drink on its ruins
And tell the story on my behalf as long as the tears flow.
How did such a love become a thing of the past,
Just another love story?

I lifted the napkin off the food and took a small piece of meat, spiced and charcoal-grilled, and raised my glass to the Baghdad sky thirteen floors up, and emptied the contents into my stomach. The Scotch was seventy years old, according to the label on the bottle, but it aged another seventy years when the lady strung out the end of the line: "*And my longing for you sears my ribs / And each second is like a burning coal of bloooooooood.*"

The customer service person in the hotel told me by phone that this kind of whisky was imported specially for people of fine taste in Baghdad and they had other kinds available, but I preferred the Scotch because we were old friends. After the fourth glass the screen started to wobble. I didn't care. I kept on sipping it, looking out on Baghdad from above. Woe on me! How had I missed this great paradise? Why had I wasted my time in that icy hell there? Why had I been so slow to come back to Baghdad? "Baghdad is paradise, guys, Baghdad is paradise," I shouted, raising my glass. I swallowed it all in one mouthful and brought the glass down on the table, and the bottle swayed in front of me. The balcony also swayed. All Baghdad had starting swaying.

"What in heaven's name is happening," I shouted at the top of my voice. I stripped off and climbed onto the table to see what had happened to the city. I saw skyscrapers dancing and about to topple over, and lampposts vibrating like the string of a bow after an arrow's been shot. I stuck my head out and looked right. The Freedom Monument was static at first, but then the brass castings on the monument started shaking too and falling off, one after another. First, the statue of the woman bending over the body of her martyred son, then the martyred son. Then the child pointing to the beginning of the road fell. My god! My god! My god! What was happening? The only thing left of the monument was the soldier that Jawad Salim, the sculptor, had given the task of breaking the bars and carrying the masses towards prosperity. What prosperity, Salim, when Baghdad was falling down? I drank the last glass from the bottle of Scotch and went back to check on the soldier. But he disappointed me. He had started trembling too. At that I threw the glass away and climbed up on the terrace, shouting, "Hang in there, Great Soldier. I'm coming."

I had decided to save him because, if the soldier fell, whole countries would fall too and turn into urinals for dogs and cats. The hotel guests heard me shouting and hurried to their balconies to see what was happening. I was completely naked, standing on the edge of the balcony, urging the soldier to hang on till I arrived. I ignored them. I closed my eyes, took a deep breath, then jumped off the balcony towards the monument, slammed into the ground and came to my senses.

"My god. Is this Baghdad?" I asked in surprise and panic.

"No. Mogadishu," Wa'il replied sarcastically.

46

Baghdad looked as if a hurricane had struck. It was devastated. The shops were falling apart and shacks were springing up along the pavements and in the streets like ants. It was covered in dust and everything in the city was the colour of sand because a dust cloud had blown in, no one knew from where, filling the city's lungs. I paid no attention to the farewells from my travelling companions on my journey from Amman or to the jokes of that young GMC driver who likened Baghdad to poor Mogadishu. I was shocked like a cat that loses its footing and falls off a tall building. My headache reappeared, screaming in my head like the electricity generators standing on the pavements outside the shops. The noise was deafening. Holding my head, I stopped and, with eyes half-closed, looked at the faces of the passers-by, people so tired they seemed to have just completed a marathon.

I took a taxi to New Baghdad and asked the driver to take me to Hamza the herbalist's shop behind the Syriac quarter, if he knew it. The man nodded, turned down the radio and said, "In you get. You can't get lost in New Baghdad." Then he turned up the radio again. He was a musical driver, tapping on the steering wheel and swaying to the song on the radio: "*Oh orange, Oh orange.*" I looked out at Baghdad through the car window, trying to distract myself from the din. What I saw was failure: the city was in a terrible state, littered with ruins and shanties. There was no new construction, no development, no prosperity, not even rubbish bins. Only the rubbish dumps were flourishing and singing like "the orange".

In fact, Baghdad had never been a Paris or a Stockholm, or even an Istanbul or a Cairo. It was a hungry city that the world, in a moment of meanness, had decided to punish for a crime it hadn't committed. The world imposed a strict blockade that caused the death of many thousands of the city's people, while hundreds of thousands of others emigrated and dispersed. With their usual arrogance, America and its allies said, "By starving them, we want to clip the wings of the regime and punish it for invading Kuwait." But the regime, the ruling family and friends of the regime didn't feel the hunger. They never went to bed without dinner. Dictatorial regimes and their cronies, their dogs and their cats, don't usually go hungry or thirsty. It was only ordinary Iraqis who wasted away in hunger and had their lives ruined by sanctions. In those times they made bread out of bran and dipped it in watery stock with little nutritional value. They bought eggs one at a time, tomato paste by the spoonful and cooking oil in pathetic little bags. Then in each town they set up an informal market for buying and selling poor-quality rice and lentils. They fed their babies on powdered formula imported from the worst places in the world, repeating the words that al-Mutanabbi the poet once spoke: "If you're drowning, getting wet is the least of your fears."

Good things were in short supply and only the flea markets flourished. Second-hand trousers and undershirts were available, as well as jackets that were made of poor-quality material and had been redyed. The pavements were also full of used furniture because many women had sold off their bedroom furniture and slept on the floor, which was hot in summer. Marital beds moved from bride to bride, to finally end up as junk that the dealers would barter for a jug made of recycled plastic. Poor people sold everything they could get their hands on, even the roofs of their houses, to buy bread for their families. One evening my mother had told me on the phone that our neighbour was celebrating because the state had decided to give people a wonderful gift: a frozen chicken in a plastic wrapper that bore the words: "A gift from the President and Leader, may God preserve and protect him".

Baghdad at that time was hungry and tired, like an orphaned child on whom no one takes pity. News of its hunger reached us abroad, and we held protests in exile and shouted at the world, to no avail. But what rubbed salt into the wounds of the tragedy was that the people who at one time had starved the city turned up later and claimed to be saving it. They made the city unsafe to live in: a playground for rival political factions, an arena without walls, where anyone could play, whenever and however they wanted.

47

I stopped one of the boys playing football in the street and asked him where Uncle Ibrahim's house might be. He pointed at a tall brick house and said, "That's Sayyed Ibrahim's house."

"So Comrade Ibrahim is now Sayyed Ibrahim? Praise be to Him who Changes Titles!" I mumbled to myself as I walked towards the house. I knocked on the door. A girl of about six, with a white cotton hijab covering her head and neck, opened the door. It was Hala, Jalal's daughter. She didn't know me, of course, because she was born many years after I left. Jalal looked out of the kitchen window. He was carrying a pistol but as soon as he saw me, he hid it behind his back. He took me into the guest room, without his old enthusiasm, and I felt another kind of alienation from the new reality. We sat down, facing each other like adversaries, overseen by a large portrait of some prominent cleric that covered one whole wall of the room. I had no doubt that in the same place I had once seen a portrait of someone else, and traces of the old frame were still visible. On the other wall there were pictures of shrines and places of pilgrimage in the holy cities of Najaf and Kerbala. On top of the television there were also small framed pictures of clerics in white and black turbans. The house suggested that Uncle Ibrahim hadn't given up his passion for putting up pictures.

A few moments later a dignified old man appeared, with trimmed beard and moustache. He was wearing a white Arab thobe and had a white cotton skullcap on his head. He greeted me with affected humility, saying, "Peace be upon you, and the mercy and blessings of God", then offered me his hand in great solemnity. I examined the man closely, and it was indeed him: Papa Aflaq, the comrade who used to go to sleep and wake up in olive-green, military-style fatigues and who was feared throughout New Baghdad for his influence. But, like a chameleon, Comrade Ibrahim had reinvented himself as the Venerable Sayyed Ibrahim. At the time I remembered some lines of folk poetry that I had seen painted on the wall of a school along the way. "A turban with seven folds, four rings on his fingers, yet one day before the fall of the regime he was dressed in green fatigues." I'm no expert on folk poetry, but as I looked at Uncle Ibrahim, I did feel that he was one of those intended. The way snakes shed their skins! I knew he had disappeared in the first days after the overthrow of the regime in Baghdad. and then reappeared in the guise of the gallant community leader who, when he worked with the regime, had supposedly saved almost two thousand young people from execution. With their usual alacrity Iraqis believed him and started calling him Sayyed Ibrahim. What short memories Iraqis have, and what kind hearts!

I ignored Uncle Ibrahim and started asking mockingly, "Whatever became of the indispensable leader, I wonder?" But the looks Uncle Ibrahim gave me suggested that a storm was imminent, like the ones that blew up between us in the old days, so I kept it short and said I couldn't stay long because I had an important appointment. After that we had lunch together and then he took his leave on the grounds that he had a party meeting at headquarters.

"So Papa Aflaq still loves party headquarters?" I whispered to Jalal jokingly, but he just closed his eyes and clenched his jaws in displeasure. I felt embarrassed and took my leave.

At the time the militias had started to take control of Baghdad neighbourhoods, and pistols with silencers often had a decisive say in the competition between them. New expressions had also entered public discourse in cafés, newspapers and radio reports: car bombs, explosive belts, IEDs, Shi'ite militias and Sunni militias. People from abroad had awoken the sleeping ghoul of sectarianism, allowed it to destroy the country and tear it apart. Then, after distracting people with hatred, they had moved on to celebrate the division of the spoils behind the walls of the Green Zone. Jalal was frightened, even if his father was powerful and had sneaked in under the cloak of an armed religious party. He cursed the Americans and the handful of Iraqi conquerors who had come in with them on the back of Abrams tanks. He cursed the day they had come to Baghdad. "The bastards, they came from the bars of London and the nightclubs of Europe and destroyed our lives," he said indignantly. As I listened, I noticed another picture on the wall of the guest room: it was one of those Iraqis who had come home on the back of the American tanks.

I tried to change the subject. I asked him about our neighbour, Hajj Zaini, and what had become of him. He said he knew nothing about him because he hadn't gone there since my mother died. But then he added: "They must have driven him out." He took a cup of tea from his wife and continued, saying the sectarian cleansing process began early in Baghdad and it was soon normal to find a neighbour you'd known for two thirds of your life standing at your door to say goodbye. It was the threatening messages, in the form of bullets in envelopes pushed under the door at night, that defined and clinched the identity of residential areas. I finally asked him about Umm Tony, the nice widow next door who used to visit us regularly and sew clothes with my mother. He said she had taken her daughters and moved to Canada.

"Amazing! Why did she do that? Umm Tony wasn't connected with any particular group," I said.

Jalal passed me the cup of tea, sat upright and answered in a tone that came across as unjustified criticism. "You don't seem to realise, sir, that the Christians were the first victims of sectarian cleansing in Baghdad."

"Really? I swear I didn't know."

"Strange. So where have you been? Asleep in the snow?"

I felt the conversation was taking an uncomfortable turn and my cousin was saying any old thing. Trying to humour him, I said, "No, I was in the bars and the nightclubs." But he didn't smile, even out of politeness. I felt that my presence was unwelcome, so I took my leave, saying I had an appointment. I walked past our house in the neighbouring district, and it was abandoned. Only the dust of time was left inside. The outer wall was falling down and the ziziphus tree in whose shade I used to read was dying of thirst. I gave a long sigh and walked on.

48

A sandstorm blew in and Baghdad looked like a thousand tonnes of powdered turmeric had been dumped on the city. The houses, the blocks of flats, the trees, the lamp posts and even the puzzled gulls on the Tigris had all turned turmeric yellow. On my way to Andalus Square I looked up at the Freedom Monument and it had gone yellow too, but the bronze castings, thank God, were still in place, and the Great Soldier was still standing proud, breaking the bars despite the stray shrapnel that had damaged his arms. I finally reached the hotel. I took my suitcase out of the taxi and bought a sim card from the kiosk outside the hotel. I inserted it in place of the Norwegian one and called Abir.

"Said? Is that you?" she said, obviously surprised.

"Yes, me," I replied in a tired voice.

"Great! When did you arrive?"

"Today, a few hours ago," I said.

"Glad you had a safe journey."

"Thanks. Shall we meet?" I asked.

"Today?"

"Yes, today. Any objection?"

"But I'm not in Baghdad now. I'm in Diyala and I

have work to do."

"Okay, when will you be back?"

"Tomorrow, because I have to get ready for the trip to al-Kifl."

"When are they going to open the grave?"

"On Sunday. You have to be ready."

"Okay. Shall we go together then?"

"No, you go on your own and I'll come with the work team and meet you there."

Before calling off, she gave me the address of the mass grave in al-Kifl and said she looked forward to seeing me. A romantic encounter on the edge of a grave! What was it about Iraq and its endless fantasies?

49

Wars grind cities down, make them look like widows bringing up a dozen orphans. Baghdad looked exhausted. The shops closed before nightfall, stray dogs roamed the backstreets, sharing plunder with the thieves. Rubbish blew over the surface of the city and miserable concrete barriers weighed on it, cutting it into pieces in the name of security requirements. The shrieking of police cars and official convoys never stopped. Every now and then I could hear the rattle of gunfire in the sky.

Close to Saadoun Street I saw some US Army units acting suspiciously. I asked Suhail, one of the hotel staff, about it, and he started telling me about the raids and arrests the Americans carried out at night, and sporadic clashes between armed factions. He was a fine young man and I invited him to come and sit with me to watch from the balcony. But he said the situation was very bad and Baghdad was sitting on a sectarian volcano that was about to erupt. Then he came close to me to say that, in order to survive, I had to carry two identity cards and show the right one depending on the sectarian affiliation of the death squad I was dealing with. When he saw how puzzled I looked, he said he was willing to help me. Something in his eyes suggested he was telling the truth, but he remembered so many stories in all their details that I was reluctant to trust him. Listening to those gruesome tales, I was frightened. Suhail said such things did not take place only at night, but even in broad daylight, in a country that was supposedly democratic.

"And what does the state do about it?" I asked in shock.

He laughed and said, "Really sir, if we had a state, would an identity card cost just ten dollars?"

I felt so naïve at the time. With all the destruction I had seen, it was quite natural that the state would wither and its prestige would be eroded. It was quite logical that a market for forged documents should flourish in Baghdad and that people like Munir the Jackal should produce fake ID cards for paltry sums. I put my hand in my pocket and gave Suhail thirty dollars for two fake identity cards, with a tip. As he left the room he said they would be ready in no more than two days, but then he remembered he would need two photographs of me, and that gave me another anxiety attack.

"Where can I get you a picture at this time of night, Suhail?" I asked.

"Don't worry, sir, we're in Saadoun Street. In the morning you'll find hundreds of shops that do instant photos," he said, shutting the door behind him.

50

It was Nizar the Devil who tempted me to frequent Saadoun Street. We were in secondary school at the time and Nizar, with his big nose and his poor grades in maths, loved the cinema. He spent his pocket money watching films and smoking cigarettes. One day he said, "Said, would you like to come to the cinema with me?" I agreed without discussion. I was well aware that there was no point in refusing: Nizar was so good at leading people astray that we called him the devil. One Friday morning we were standing outside the Atlas cinema, along with Amjad Abbas, a young man with a talent for drawing and writing poetry.

Saadoun Street was packed with cinemas and theatres,

and crowded with restaurants, clothes shops and photo labs. That day we saw an Egyptian film called *The Monsters* and after the film Amjad suggested we have a group picture taken in one of the photo shops. I remember crossing the street to a fancy studio with dozens of colour photos in the front window. We asked the photographer to take a picture of us all together. He pointed towards a room with a narrow wooden door and said, "This way, please." The lights pointed towards a wall completely covered with a picture of a Caribbean beach with tall, elegant palm trees. The photographer placed Nizar, the tallest of us three, on a green plastic chair and had us stand behind him with our hands on his shoulders as a mark of friendship. Then he pressed the button on a small Kodak camera and said, "Come back next Friday to pick up the picture." We walked back towards Rashid Street and had shawarma sandwiches and raisin juice from Hajj Zabala's shop. Then we went back to New Baghdad, quite delighted with ourselves. It didn't end there. We started coming to Saadoun Street every week to see a film, hang out, and harass the beggars, of whom there were few despite the war. Those days gave me a love for cinema and made me save up so that I could buy a ticket and a sandwich.

One rainy autumn day we were hanging around in Rashid Street and we had to take shelter from the rain in al-Zahawi's café there. The customers in the café were gathered around someone, and curiosity drew us towards them. The someone was a dignified man in his fifties in a thick jacket and a flat cap of the kind that intellectuals commonly liked to wear at the time. He was holding a Parker 45 pen and signing identical books that the others were holding. I learned from the café owner that the man was a famous author and he was signing copies of his new novel. I stood in line with them and asked him to sign for me. "Shall I sign on your shirt? Where's your book, boy?" he said with a laugh. I was embarrassed when the others chuckled, but the writer quickly changed his tone. "Never mind, I'll give you a copy for free," he said. He took a book out of a shoulder bag lying nearby and signed it with a beautiful greeting on the first page. "Here you are, read it and enjoy." This was the first novel I ever owned and it made me a compulsive reader that dreamed of studying literature. When I finished the book, I felt that Nizar the Devil had not only tempted me to visit Saadoun Street and love the cinema. He was also the reason why I loved to have books. But that passion of mine would dismay my mother. Whenever she saw a book in my hands she got frightened and thought of my father's fate. The government didn't like people who read books, she said.

I have no idea what became of Nizar the Devil or the people who went to the Atlas cinema, which is now abandoned and in ruins. I crossed to the other side of the street looking for a studio that would take my picture. The pavements were clogged with carts selling cheap goods and the sellers were crying their wares through little loudspeakers. "Everything for a quarter, everything for a quarter, everything for a quarter," one of them shouted. Despite the noise, I could see the anxiety in the faces of the people passing. Dozens of bombs had exploded in Saadoun Street and dozens of people had met their demise on its pavements. It was especially dangerous there because more official cars drove by in a single day than anywhere else in the country. I had a close look at the statue of Abdul Muhsin al-Saadoun and it looked like someone had daubed black paint on it with a brush and then sprayed it with a coat of cheap varnish. Suhail told me later that the statue I saw was a replica. The real statue had been stolen two years earlier and had been replaced, like many other statues in Baghdad. At the time the whole country was a playground for gangs that stole and smuggled out antiquities and anything of value.

My steps took me to Kaka Ali's kebab restaurant and I found myself unconsciously walking through the doorway and ordering three skewers of kebab and a whole roasted onion of the kind that is indispensable with any kebab. The smell of meat sizzling over hot coals was pungent and evocative. I remembered my mother feeding chunks of meat into a small manual mincing machine and turning the meat into kebabs that tasted as good as the famous Sulaymaniyah kebabs. She would wake me up early on Fridays to fetch loaves of bread from the bakery near our house. On my way back I would nibble the ends of a loaf, then put it back in the bag. When she saw the nibbled bread. she would fly into a rage at me, then calm down and smile.

The waiter brought the skewers of kebab on a plate alongside a tomato grilled on the coals, a whole roast onion, as I had ordered, and half a bitter orange. Then he put a basket of bread straight from the oven onto the table.

"Need anything else, sir?" he asked.

"No, thanks."

But then I remembered that at the door I had seen a large container of my favourite Erbil yoghurt with ice cubes floating on the surface, so I called him back.

"Excuse me . . ."

"Yes, sir."

"I'll have a yoghurt too, please."

"Coming up."

"Thanks."

I sprinkled the kebab with sumac and squeezed the half orange onto it, then I picked up some bread and performed one of my sacred rituals. In Norway I did eat kebabs, but they didn't taste the same as the kebabs in the backstreets of Baghdad. Besides, kebabs don't suit fancy restaurants with gilt tables or soft jazz music. Kebabs are a people's dish, which tastes best in small, crowded restaurants, and they're delicious when they coupled with romantic songs on the radio. "There you are, sir," said the waiter, putting a wonderful glass of yoghurt in front of me. My god, how delicious it was with the kebab!

I finished my meal, paid the bill and left. At the door I

bought a cup of tea from a brown-skinned youth who was standing at a small cart with the words "This is from the grace of my Lord" painted on the side. He spoke in a lovely southern accent. I thought he was from Maysan but he said he was from Nasiriyah. "It makes no difference. We're all Iraqis," he added. I wish they could hear you, those idiots lurking behind the barricades of sectarianism, and learn from you, you kind-hearted and hard-working young man.

I walked on to Tahrir Square, then turned right to a shop that did instant photos. I asked the owner about photos with a white background for official purposes. He said it wouldn't take more than ten minutes and took me into a small room. In a matter of seconds he sat me down in front of a modern Canon camera attached to a black metal arm and took a picture of me. Then he went off to Photoshop out all the effects of age and give the photo a white background. But then there was a power cut and the surge protection device started to whistle. The man slammed his fist on the table in front of him and cursed the day when God decided to make him Iraqi. Then, grumbling, he pulled the cord on the generator that stood by the door. The generator wasn't powerful enough to run the air conditioning, which meant the studio was soon like a Turkish bath. Suddenly, the noise died down and the generator came to a halt. He remembered that he hadn't filled it with petrol. He borrowed two litres from his neighbour, poured them into the tank and soon had it chugging away again. But the back-up power had stopped so the photo had to be redone. The process had taken a whole hour, and in the meantime, we had inhaled enough exhaust fumes to asphyxiate a herd of elephants. Finally, the photographer handed me a small white envelope, with four photos against a white background, in exchange for next to nothing. Then I walked across Tahrir Square towards Bab al-Sharqi. It was Friday and very crowded there. The shops and streets were full of people shopping and the pavements were teeming with carts selling pills, fake Viagra and packets of condoms. Between the carts there were tables stacked with hundreds of bootleg DVDs of pornographic films. Bab al-Sharqi was now a centre for people selling drugs and porn films and gamblers. As you walked through, you had to watch out for pickpockets and steer clear of the gangs gathered around hustlers playing the three-card trick.

I walked on towards al-Khilani Square and al-Khulafa Street. The shops were full of Chinese goods. The whole city might as well have had "Made in China" stamped on its forehead. The lamps, the carpets, the pots and pans, the pens and the notebooks were all from China. Even the singing birds in the Ghazil pet market were displayed in flimsy Chinese cages instead of the palm-frond cages they used to have. Near the Shorja market I even saw someone selling wooden chopsticks and the Chinese characters on them looked like those curly zalabia. I was curious to know who was buying chopsticks in a city that likes to eat kebabs and dolma.

The man smiled and said, "They buy them to scratch their backs." I laughed at his sense of humour and bought one from him, then walked on towards Rashid Street.

Broken, dust-strewn pavements and tiles falling out like children's milk teeth. The shops and buildings on each side of the street looked tired and decrepit. Generator wires trailed all over them and made them look shabby. As for the pillars in the colonnades for which this ancient street was famous, they had been plastered with advertisements. Rashid Street was a shocking sight. There were piles of rubbish and stray cats and dogs roaming everywhere unmolested. I saw two dogs mating casually and undaunted under the statue of Ma'ruf al-Rusafi the poet. Rusafi could hear them panting as, in stony silence, he watched a giant tide of rubbish advancing towards him. The wall of the Haydar-Khana mosque carried so many death notices that it looked black, the colour of sorrow. "God has promised truly," the posters invariably began. "Verily we are God's and to Him we return," they ended. They were just like the commemorative strips of black cloth we used to see all over the walls twenty years earlier: the ink never dries on Baghdad's death notices. In one of the local newspapers on display at a kiosk I read that the death toll for the month was six hundred and seventy-two Iraqis. Men, women and children slain by car bombs and in other explosions, for no fault other than being born on this piece of land. I had a cup of tea in al-

Zahawi's café and turned into al-Mutanabbi Street, where the bookshops are, before returning. You've missed much if you haven't visited this street on a Friday, but it was in no better condition than the other streets. Waste paper and cigarette butts littered the sides of the street and made it look even more miserable. I stopped at a man who had stacked a pile of old books on the pavement, with a little sign saying "Five for 1,000 dinars". These were personal libraries that people had inherited but were not interested in keeping, so they sold them off to the dealers, who piled them high on the pavement. I crouched down and started to look through the books in search of rare signed copies. In the end I came across a copy of *The Drowned Temple*, al-Sayyab's collection of poems, published in Beirut by Dar al-Ilm lil-Malayin, and on the inside page the author had written a dedication to his poet friend, Hussein Mardan. I can't imagine how anyone could throw away a book with such a dedication. I paid the man ten thousand dinars, instead of the thousand he had asked for, and retraced my steps to the hotel.

On the way back, I noticed a death notice on the wall of the Baghdad Municipality building: "God has promised truly. Baghdad Municipality mourns the passing of Martyr Engineer Jamal al-Saadoun, who was killed in a cowardly assassination on June 21, 2005. Verily we are God's and to Him we shall return."

51

Ali and Omar, two names I never imagined I would share, given to me by a Baghdad forger for thirty dollars and a tip, because death squads had started to proliferate in the city like lice in a tramp's hair and one never knew when a bunch of masked men might appear, block your way and ask you to prove you were Shi'ite Ali rather than Sunni Omar, or vice versa. The identity card war had started in earnest: the Ali v Omar game, on which millions of dollars were spent, would cost the lives of many Iraqis, especially those who only had one identity card in their pockets. Even those who carried alternative ID cards were not safe if they couldn't guess the sectarian affiliation of the people standing in their way. How many Omars showed Ali's ID card on the roads of death and ended up as headless corpses? How many Alis took out Omar's ID card in the wrong place and ended up as history?

I picked up the picture frame and had a long look at it, torn between two emotions: happiness at the idea of seeing my father and fear that he might vanish, as on previous occasions. But first I had to be lucky enough to get there, because between Baghdad and al-Kifl there were many trouble spots, many freelance gangs and ruthless killers. I still wasn't confident I could pass the ID test and survive, but what strengthened my resolve and helped me resist my fears was the fact that I would finally find out what my father looked like. How I had waited for that moment! I would take photographs of him with my camera and put the picture, something that had always been missing from my life, inside this frame. Then I would hang it on the wall in my study.

52

There was a noise from the corridor that sounded like the tambourines played in funeral processions. I sat there anxiously, anticipating the next beat, but eventually it stopped. I looked up and saw masked men and a preacher in a small white turban, with a Qur'an under his arm. "Come on, up you get," one of the masked men said. I couldn't get up, so they grabbed me and hauled me off to another room. My feet dragged along the floor, leaving a trail that told the whole story. They took me up to the scaffold and put a black cloth bag over my head. They wrapped a thick rope around my neck and tightened it until it squeaked like poor people's beds. Then the preacher made various predictably derogatory remarks about me. He stepped down off the scaffold platform and stood in line near the prison governor. The governor read the execution proclamation in a booming voice and then shouted, "Carry out the execution!" One of the executioners pulled down the lever, saying "In the name of God . . ." and a wooden trapdoor opened under my feet, and I dangled there like a hanged cat. I came to my senses and found the frame was still in my hand and my shoulder bag was open. I shoved the frame into the bag along with the camera and the charger, set the alarm clock for seven a.m. and went to bed.

53

"Please, how can I get to al-Kifl?" I asked a stranger at the Allawi station, and he said I should go to Hillah first and then go on to al-Kifl. Kindly, he pointed at a Kia minibus and said it was going to Hillah. With my arrival, the car had enough passengers to leave. I put my bag on my lap and squeezed in between two talkative men who were smoking voraciously.

It isn't far from Baghdad to Hillah but the road isn't safe. That's what I was told by both Suhail and the Kia driver who, as he changed gear and pressed the accelerator, had much to say about sectarian killings.

The intrepid driver and the two men beside me traded stories about masked men who suddenly appeared on the road like hungry wolves and the highly professional ambushes they laid for travellers, but I was less worried about being ambushed than about being unable to recognise my father's body. I had to meet Abir there because she would help me do that. She had dealt with dead people many times and, because of the nature of her work, she had covered many mass graves and written dozens of news stories about the things she had seen, filing them away under the title: Iraqi's Tragedy of Pain. The number of mass graves discovered had reached about three hundred and fifty, some of which held hundreds of innocent and admirable Iraqis.

She once told me about the largest mass grave discovered after the fall of the Saddam regime in 2003. It was in the village of Abu Sudayra, just a few miles from the historic town of Babylon. It held two thousand, eight hundred bodies, buried there in 1991. The bodies were completely decomposed, except for skulls and bones, tufts of hair and scraps of cloth. People came to the grave from all over the country, gathered around the bones laid out on plastic sheeting, and started weeping and wailing. Fathers counted the bones of their sons with an equanimity that even camels wouldn't have been able to muster. Whenever one of the mothers found the bones of a relative she and her friends formed circles and scattered dust on their heads in mourning.

Abir says she saw an elderly man in Arab dress,

including a keffiyeh with an agal, who seemed moved and extremely sad. He was squatting, staring at a skull and some bones, including a thigh bone, and puffing away anxiously on a cigarette. She moved closer out of curiosity and waited till he had finished his cigarette. Then the man put his hand in his pocket, took out a plastic bag and put the skull and bones into it. He was about to leave, but she went up to him and brought out a tape recorder in the hope of a quick interview.

"Please, sir, I have a question if you would."

"Sure."

"Have you come looking for someone's body in this grave?"

"Yes, the body of Majid, my son."

"And did you find it?"

"Yes, here it is," he said glumly, lifting up the bag.

"And how can you be sure that it's your son's?"

The man gave a deep sigh and said, "To tell you the truth, miss, I can't be sure these bones are Majid's, but a few years ago, when his mother was dying, I promised her I would find him and bury him by her side, and I fear I may die before I've had a chance to keep my promise."

The man picked up the bag of bones and left.

54

"Get your ID cards ready. Checkpoint ahead," said the minibus driver. "This is Latifiya. Fingers crossed."

There were five masked men in military fatigues without insignia, carrying Kalashnikovs and blocking the road with rocks. On the side of the road stood a pick-up truck, with nothing to show it was a government vehicle. The truck had no licence plates and the sides had been spray-painted badly. One of the men came up to us. "Give us your ID cards, and quickly," he ordered gruffly. I remembered Suhail's instructions, but which identity card should I show them in Latifiya? The driver handed the man his ID card first. The man examined it, then handed it back. The passenger in the front was a little slow, so the masked man turned to us. The men beside me offered him their cards. He took them, examined the names and gave them back, wishing them well. Then it was my turn. I closed my eyes, put my hand in my shirt pocket and took out the card that was there. The masked man took it. He looked back and forth between me and the card. The way he looked at me made my stomach clench in fear and I almost fainted. I wasn't sure which card I should have shown him: the one in my shirt pocket or the one in my wallet in the back pocket of my trousers? Omar or Ali?

"Omar?" the man said.

"Yes," I replied with as much composure as I could manage.

"Here you are, brother, have a good day."

So, I had survived and the identity card hadn't been exposed as a fake. The man moved on to the third row of seats and then the fourth. Now there was just the passenger in the front. "Your ID card, please. Let's get this over with," said the man. The passenger gave him his ID card. The man read the name and aggressively told the passenger to get out. He handcuffed the man and took him off to the pick-up truck. Then he waved us on. Apparently, the poor passenger didn't have what he needed to save him from a violent death. What a tragic fate! An identity card had decided between life and death. God damn identity cards.

I took my Ali ID card out of my wallet and stuffed it in my left sock in case I was searched at another checkpoint and my secret exposed. I was going to spend the rest of this journey as Omar rather than Ali. One of my talkative neighbours gave me a funny look but I didn't care. I looked out at the villages as the minibus zipped past them one by one. I read a sign with an arrow pointing right: "This way to the ancient city of Babylon" it said. A flood of memories came to the surface when I saw the name Babylon. I remembered my history teacher, Mr Abdel Bari, who took us on a trip twenty-two years ago to the Land of God, as he called it. He was in his mid-thirties, medium height, neat with glasses and a long nose. He not only remembered our names, but the full names of all six hundred boys in the Tadamun Secondary School. He coached us for our football matches against other schools although he taught history, not physical education.

When we set foot in Babylon for the first time, he told us it was haunted by the spirits of the Amorites and we should keep well away from each other when we walked among the ruins. I remember feeling frightened when I walked through the Ishtar Gate that day. It was a massive structure, dressed with blue-glazed bricks and decorated with images of lions, aurochs and dragons in low relief. He said the animals were symbols of the many gods our ancestors believed in. The lion was the symbol of the goddess Ishtar and the aurochs the symbol of Adad. As for the dragons, which they called *mushkhushshu*, they were the symbol of the god Marduk. Once the teacher had given his explanation, we lined up for an itinerant photographer who took a Polaroid picture of us. He waved it around in the air until the details appeared. We walked on, passing the photo around and laughing at the way we looked in the picture, which would gather dust in the school archives. Then we went to the main square, to find the statue of a mighty lion, mounted on a stone plinth, with a man prostrate between its legs. "Follow me to have a taste of history," Mr Abdel Bari shouted, pointing towards the Hanging Gardens of Babylon. We followed, impatient to see one of the seven wonders of the ancient world. His hands laced across his chest, he proudly told us a story. "One day your ancestor, Nebuchadnezzar, was sitting at home with his wife and she complained to him about the landscape in Babylon. She said she found it boring and she longed for Fars, where the land was green and hilly. Her loving husband ordered the construction of hanging gardens that would remind her of life in the land of her forefathers. He brought dozens of architects and thousands of builders and craftsmen to work on the project. They built terraces on different levels, connected to each other by marble stairways supported on marble arches. They even built gardens raised from the ground on marble columns and alongside the terraces they dug out ponds lined with lead, surrounded by a massive wall, and in it they planted decorative flowers and other plants. Then they installed screw pumps to lift the water from the Euphrates and channel it into the gardens and the upper terraces. Have you ever seen anything more wonderful than that?"

This story gave us great inspiration, but in reality we couldn't taste the history that our teacher spoke about so proudly, because these monuments had been refaced with modern "republican" bricks and looked as if they had been built the previous Saturday. We told him this, but he stuck to his line, possibly because he was worried about any challenge to the authorised version of history. Probably the walls of Babylon also had ears, like the walls everywhere else in Iraq. If the walls had been deaf, the man would have shouted so loud that all the ugly modern bricks that covered the ancient walls would have fallen off. The regime had launched a "modernisation" revolution with its stupid modern bricks in Babylon, leading UNESCO to withhold approval of Iraq's application to have Babylon designated as a world heritage site. In Saddam Hussein's time three palaces were built among the ruins, with some of the bricks inscribed with his initials, S H, and with a large tarmacked car park. Then giant oil pipelines were built across the site. The United States appeared in the Land of God to continue the chain of destruction. Tracked vehicles and Abrams tanks drove over the processional way where the kings, priests and people of great Babylon had walked before them. Archaeological remains were crushed and the earthen berms that the troops built were full of pottery shards and clay tablets with cuneiform writing. Thanks to the United States, fifteen archaeological sites were dug up and plundered and the Iraq Museum in Baghdad was looted while US troops looked on, with thousands of ancient artefacts smuggled abroad.

I don't think Mr Abdel Bari ever found out what happened to the Land of God that he loved, and whose picture he had hanging up in the staff room at school. He was captured by the Iranians and, at the time of writing, had not yet been set free.

We finally reached al-Hilla. I got my bag out and bought a bottle of mineral water from a small kiosk at the entrance to the bus station. Then I found a taxi to take me to the place where they were opening the mass grave of "militants" in al-Kifl. The driver wasn't happy when he heard the word "militants", as if someone had insulted his ancestors. It was a small graveyard about three hundred yards beyond the tomb of the Prophet Ezekiel. When I got there, I saw men gathered around a hole in the ground and women beating their breasts and wailing at the top of their voices. I went closer and no one showed any interest in me. The volunteers were busy recovering skulls and bones and the other men were waiting to identify the remains of their relatives. A digging machine had opened a small trench, while the volunteers and some of the relatives were digging away with picks and with their bare hands. When I arrived they had recovered nineteen incomplete bodies. The piles of bones had no identity papers because the grave was more than thirty years old and no identity papers would last that long.

The day passed and Abir's team had still not turned up. I tried calling her mobile phone but all I got was a recorded message saying that her phone was turned off or out of network coverage. I finished a whole packet of cigarettes as I walked around the pile of bones with my camera hanging around my neck ready for a picture I had waited all my life to take. I approached a Red Crescent official in the hope he might help me identify my father's remains. He asked me to be patient, saying the work wasn't over yet and they were still looking for more bodies. Where could I find this patience? I waited on tenterhooks until the digging work was complete and the last bone had been brought out. Then the bodies were laid out in lines on white or black plastic sheeting and each body was given a number. Then the people standing around were allowed to identify their relatives and wrap them in shrouds. The holes in the skulls were full of soil and they had put a set of bones under each skull. I saw some young men gathering their fathers' bones in plastic bags and pieces of cloth and going to the Red Crescent official to sign receipts.

There was nothing to confirm that the bones were really those of their relatives, but after waiting thirty-seven years they were convinced, and content with the handful of bones they had managed to retrieve. They were certain their fathers wouldn't come back to life and they knew they had to build tombs for them and weep over them, since tombs, even if the bones are not authentic, tend to help people reach closure and ease the pain of their loss. It's selfishness in its most obvious form: we stuff our loved ones into graves to alleviate the grief in our hearts and go back to living again. That's what I muttered as I watched everyone hurrying off with their bags towards the cemetery, including a dignified old man. "Why are you so keen to bury him in a separate, specially constructed tomb?" I asked him.

"When you don't have a tombstone, you die twice," he said dejectedly. "Once when your life ends, and a second time when you're forgotten and no one remembers you."

The sun was about to set, people started to leave and there were fewer and fewer bodies on display. Close to losing hope, I went up to a medium-sized skull lying close to a pile of bones on one of the plastic sheets. I crouched down and picked it up, turned it over and started counting the holes: one hole, two holes, three. It had been buried alive so there was no bullet hole in it. I examined it carefully. There was a strip of metal wire connecting the teeth. I had a feeling this skeleton was the one for me. I put it back in its place, and laid out the bones underneath it. I had obtained an incomplete father. I took a picture of him, then put him in a black plastic bag, picked it up and left.

55

The town was sunk in darkness and the road to Baghdad would not be safe by night. I looked at the sky and the moon was as pale as the faces of the dead. A dark grey cloud crept towards it. I was alone, walking aimlessly in the dark, carrying my father's remains in a black bag and singing, "O you who lie underground, I've come to mourn my love for those I've loved." I saw the lights of a car in the distance. When it came nearer, I stopped and waved it down. It was a Toyota Crown taxi with a drunken driver. I told him I was a stranger in town and asked him to take me to Hillah and show me the way to a hotel where I could spend the night. "Okay, in you get," he said. I got in, clutching my bag of bones to my chest, and we drove north towards al-Hilla. The driver handed me a bottle of arak. "Help yourself. This is vintage arak," he said. "Who will revive the bones when they are old and decayed?" he added in jest, quoting the Qur'an. I thanked him and kept quiet. The driver was in his late fifties, clean shaven, wearing a white dishdasha strewn with the husks of the sunflower seeds he'd been eating. On his head he had a white knitted cap. He seemed relaxed, as if he were in a bar drinking arak and eating nuts. But when he saw a lamp flashing intermittently in the distance he looked anxious and wasn't sure exactly what to do. Should he put on the brakes, press the accelerator, or turn around and go back? He threw the arak bottle out of the window, put a small handful of cardamom pods in his mouth and started chewing them, mumbling a prayer asking God to save us from the devil. After that he recited a verse of the Qur'an thought to bring about invisibility: "We have set up barriers in front of them and behind them and have screened them off so that they cannot see." He repeated it with such reverence that I thought God was going to grant him wings to fly away like an angel or urgently send him a cloak of invisibility to save him from his predicament.

I didn't know exactly why the driver was suddenly so

agitated or what the flashing signal might mean, but the state the man was in suggested we were in trouble. We drove up to the light and found it was a temporary checkpoint made with stones on the road, checking ID cards. There were two masked soldiers, with no insignia of rank, each with a lantern and a Kalashnikov rifle. On the side of the road there was a pick-up truck with no licence plates, badly painted like the one earlier in the day. "Identity cards," one of them said, pointing his gun at the driver. The suddenly repentant driver handed him his card. The soldier read it in the lamp light and handed it back. Then he asked me for mine and I handed it to him with some peace of mind. But when he read it, he banged on the side of the taxi and said, "Get out." I got out of the taxi with my bag of bones. Two masked men, armed to the teeth, jumped out of the pick-up. One of them twisted my arms back and handcuffed me. They threw me deftly onto the open bed at the back of the pick-up and drove off with me at high speed, tyres screeching. I wished I had drunk some of the driver's arak and mumbled the same prayer when we saw them. On the way one of the men confiscated my mobile phone and my shoulder bag. Then he took the black plastic bag to see what was in it. But just at that moment the pick-up hit a large bump in the road and the bag flew out of the man's hands and the contents were scattered on the roadway. In the meantime, a truck came along and ran over the skull and the bones.

I heard my father screaming as his head was crushed

under the wheels of the truck. I called out to my captors to stop so that I could pick up the fragments, but one of them silenced me with a kick in the mouth. Then he blindfolded me and threatened to kill me if I opened my mouth again. The truck drove for many miles, along paved and unpaved roads, until we reached an area where there was complete silence and not a sign of life. Death alone walked there and spent the night in whatever basements or dungeons it fancied.

My captors took me out of the truck and walked me a few yards. One of them opened a metal door that was chained and locked. The door made a squeak as frightening as the eyes of a demon in a dark room. One of the men slapped me as he pushed me inside. I rolled down some worn stone stairs and fell into a damp and stifling underground room. The kidnappers went out, locked the door with the chain and left. Still blindfolded, I could hear mice and insects crawling towards me. "Oh my god, where am I? And who are these bastards? What do they want from me?" Question marks lit up in my head and I repeated the questions in a low voice for fear the walls might have ears.

In the morning I heard the door opening. I was lying on the floor almost dead from thirst and fear. Someone grabbed me by the shoulders and sat me up. He gave me a little water to drink, then gave me a welcoming slap on the back of my neck. "Welcome, Omar. Welcome, you son of a whore," he said.

From the way he greeted me, I realised who I was

dealing with and which identity card I should have shown them.

"I'm not Omar," I said, my eyes still blindfolded because my hands were tied behind my back.

"Shut up or else I'll fill your mouth with shit," he replied, then slapped me again and left.

56

His head was smashed up and his eyes were dangling down on his cheeks. With his only hand he was holding a broken femur. He was blowing a stream of hot air from deep inside him. He came towards me as if he wanted to know what was happening. I was about to tell him the whole story, but the roof of the cell collapsed and I came around. My eyes were still blindfolded and the rats were still moving around.

57

The next day someone took the blindfold off my eyes. A thin ray of sunlight poured into my cell through a small hole in the ceiling, lighting up the specks of dust. I followed the sunbeam to the end and found it fell on the face of a surly young man no more than twenty years old, holding a Kalashnikov with a wooden stock. Nearby another young man with a black headscarf was waving a 9 mm pistol. They were hardly old enough to carry weapons or carry out interrogations.

"Is your name Omar?" the man in the headscarf asked.

"No," I replied.

"So what is your name?"

"Ali."

"But your ID card says Omar!"

"Because it's a fake ID."

They laughed, and the surly one kicked me and asked me to answer the questions without beating about the bush. I swore I wasn't called Omar and told them about the other ID card in my left sock. He took it out after kicking me twice in the waist. He started to read from the card, but he didn't sound very convinced:

"Name: Ali, Name of Father and Grandfather: Abdel Amid Salman, Family Name: Al-Niama, Name of

Mother and Maternal Grandfather: Naziha Jassim, Gender: Male."

"Male duck more like it," the other one commented with a laugh. Then he turned the card over and continued reading:

"Profession: Businessman, Religion and Faith: Muslim, Date of Birth: 13/5/1968, Place of Birth: Baghdad/al-Rusafa/al-Shu'la District."

He threw the ID card aside, hit me on the back of the neck and said, "Son of a bitch, think you can make fools of us?"

I felt that the Ali card had made the men even more suspicious and they started kicking me. After thirteen thousand and one kicks, the man in the headscarf crouched down and stuck his yellow face in front of mine and, spelling out each syllable one by one, asked, "Who – sent – you – to – us?"

"No one sent me, believe me. Besides who are you exactly and why am I here?" I replied.

"Shut up and answer the question," he said.

Then he tried asking the question in a different form: "How much did America pay you to spy on us?"

Ah, so the accusation was ready-made then: spying for America, the same America we had demonstrated against in exile. Oh, the irony of fate! I didn't say a word in response. I couldn't take in what he was saying. What kind of spying was this young man talking about in the age of drones? And what kind of spy would America send to a cemetery when the cameras in their satellites could count the hairs on the nose of a goat hiding in a cave?

"Son a bitch, struck deaf, are we?" shouted the surly one as he struck me on the forehead with the stock of his rifle. I fell backwards and blood ran over my eyes. The man with the headscarf sat me up again and asked me to confess before they carried out the sentence of God and his prophet.

I don't know who gave this young man with foul breath the right to argue the case for God and his prophet. Where did he get the password to log on to God's account and find out what he did and didn't mean by his sharia? And what kind of law was it that allowed young men to abduct, abuse and humiliate defenceless people? I told him the whole story but he didn't believe it. At the end of it he spat in my face, and he and his assistant went off like any other lowlifes. In the evening his assistant came back with another man, no less surly and unpleasant. They locked the door from the inside and launched into a serious bout of kicking, whipping and cursing. They beat me mercilessly as if there were a thousand-year-old vendetta between us. I was at their feet screaming for mercy, but it was no use, since vendetta beatings don't tend to end quickly. One of the men jumped in the air and then brought his boots down on my stomach. I threw up and started to cough. The other man lit a cigarette and started playing at stubbing it out on my back and my hands. Then he pulled down his pants and rinsed my face in a stream of urine. They filled my mouth with a handful of wet soil. They cursed my father, my mother, Norway, America, Adidas and McDonald's restaurants. They wanted to extract a confession that I was spying for the US Army or for some militia group. I shouted a thousand times that the accusation was baseless and ridiculous. I yelled another thousand times that I had nothing to do with America and didn't belong to any party, organisation or armed group. I swore by a thousand prophets at rest in their graves, by a thousand imams whose tombs are visited by pilgrims and by ten thousand henna-daubed mausoleums that I was just an expatriate citizen unaffiliated to any organisation who had come looking for his father's remains, and nothing more. But it was pointless: people of this kind are suspicious by nature, instinctively sceptical. In the end one of the men picked up one of the Kalashnikovs leaning against the wall and punched me in the chest with the butt. Then the two of them spat at me and left.

58

The rats ceased their frenetic activity and an eerie silence descended on my cell. I opened my eyes with great difficulty in an attempt to see beyond the dried blood that covered them. I saw someone lying nearby. I called to him but he didn't answer. He was in the foetal position and his body was covered with blood. At first, I thought he was another victim of the sharia kids, the protectors of the sharia's honour, and had been brought to the cell without me noticing. I crawled towards him and took the blindfold off his eyes. He stood up like a giant. His face was such a mess I thought a mine must have exploded in his face. He took a step back. "Where's my grave?" he said, in a voice that came from his chest. I reached out to hold him and pull myself up but he vanished, and I came to my senses. The day was almost over and no one had come yet. The temperature was above 50 degrees Celsius and it was like a frying pan in the cell. I thought I would die of thirst and be buried there, never to be heard of again. What a wretched fate – to be taken from a safe apartment in the far north of the world and end up thousands of miles away, thrown into this scorching hell.

Finally, I heard the cell door opening. Three men came down the stairs – the man with the yellow face, the one with the black keffiyeh, and his surly, putrid assistant. I was lying on the ground like a puppy dog under attack by street kids, covered in dust mixed with sweat and blood. The assistant made me sit up. The man in the keffiyeh read out a proclamation sentencing me to death and ordered that the sentence be carried out immediately. The third man pulled at my chains, then grabbed my shoulder and pointed a gun at my head to make me kneel. I didn't put up any resistance or make any plea for mercy, because at that moment death would have been a gift from heaven, a relief from pain and humiliation. With the gun to my head, I remembered what Abir had said: "Iraq is paradise, Said," and I let out an involuntary laugh. The man with the gun was squeezing the trigger but the old man put his hand over the muzzle of the gun, pushed the man aside and knelt down in front of me. "So you're not a spy, Omar?" he said.

"No, I swear I'm not a spy, and I'm not Omar, or Ali."

"So who are you? And what are you doing in our territory?"

I swallowed some saliva mixed with blood and soil, and turned to face him. I had a feeling he believed me and I was going to survive. "My name's Said Nassir Mardan. I came from Norway to Iraq to look for my father's body in a mass grave. If you don't believe, turn on the camera and check."

He gave me some water to drink from a bottle he had and told one of his friends to fetch the camera from their vehicle. When he brought it back, the old man tried to turn it on but he couldn't, so he handed it to me. I turned it on and showed him the only picture that was in it. "See, this is my father," I said.

The young man looked in amazement at the handful of bones lined up under a skull stuffed with soil. He turned it off and intoned: "There is no power or strength but through God on high, the Almighty." But then he whispered in my ear, "I'll come back to kill you", and left with his two companions. Late that night someone came in dark glasses and with the rest of his face masked. He untied me, gave me my camera, phone and wallet, which had been emptied out, no doubt through some sharia-compliant process. Then he took me out of the cellar and said, "Kneel and don't turn around till you can no longer hear the car engine. Then run away that way. They've decided to carry out the execution tomorrow morning."

The sound of the car engine eventually died away. I looked around and found I was in the middle of a large cemetery: a stranger, barefoot and bloodied. I put my hand in my bag and took out the mobile phone to call Abir and ask her to send someone to help me, but the battery was flat. All I could see was graves, with dogs barking far away. In the end I decided to walk in the direction the last masked man had shown me, taking a distant lamp as my landmark.

59

Walking among the graves, I remembered my old neighbour, Jakob Jondal. At the time Oslo city council had given me a small flat on the ninth floor of the Venus building, a block designed for retired and elderly people in the middle of the suburb of Hellerud, to the east of the city centre. Even now I don't understand why, of all the hundreds of buildings that grace the face of the city, they chose this one for me. I was the only young person there and Jakob, who was eighty-two, had the flat right next to mine. I knocked on his door the day I arrived, to say hello and introduce myself.

"Good morning, Mr Jondal. I'm Said, your new neighbour," I said.

"Good morning, pleased to meet, Mr Sa . . ."

"Said, my name's Sa'eed," I said, adjusting the way I said the name to make it easier for a Norwegian to understand it.

"Pleased to meet you, Sa'eed."

It's the ultimate humiliation, having to mispronounce your own name so that others understand it. Sa'eed! What a horror!

Mr Jondal later told me he was planning to throw

away some furniture he no longer needed and asked me to help him move it. I agreed. Getting rid of old furniture, appliances and mattresses comes at a cost in Norway. You have to take the stuff to a recycling centre and pay for disposal. You're liable to be fined if you try dumping it in the street. I rented a van and loaded it with the stuff Jakob had decided to get rid of, then I took it to the rubbish dump. At the time he gave me an elegant lamp and a bowl of cherries as a token of gratitude and good neighbourliness. After that he would knock on my door whenever he had the urge to feel he was still alive. For two whole years I never saw anyone visit him, although he had three sons and two sisters. He told me he celebrated his birthday alone and his sons just gave him their birthday greetings on the phone. After that I started organising a little birthday party for him, inviting the other old people on the ninth floor. On holidays, when the weather was spring-like, I would bake a cake, make a thermos of tea and take him for a picnic in the park.

One day I woke up to the sound of an ambulance at the entrance to the building. I hurried to the window and saw the paramedics sliding a white stretcher into the back of the ambulance, with Jakob Jandal lying on it as confident as someone who was sure they had passed their high school exams. The cleaner had found him dead in his rocking chair in the sitting room. I remember that I covered his lamp that evening with a piece of black cloth, in mourning for him. Then I went to the cemetery and put a bouquet of flowers on his neat grave in the cherry orchard.

Jacob had bought a cherry orchard on the edge of the city when he reached the age of eighty-six and said in his will that he should be buried there on his death. At the time I asked him why he wanted to be buried there.

Chewing a cherry slowly and with relish, he said, "There's an old legend that says that when you die you turn into something that matches your surroundings. If you're buried in the mountains, you turn into a rock. If you're buried in the sea, you turn into a fish, and if you're buried in the desert, you turn into sand. So I've decided to be buried in a cherry orchard so that I turn into a cherry tree. Glory to those at rest in the cherry orchard."

I don't know whether my kindly neighbour's body has yet decomposed and turned into a cherry tree, but I'm confident that his soul is resting in peace and quiet in that orchard.

Ah, if it wasn't for the despots, my father would now be at rest in a grave like that of Jakob Jondal. Maybe he would have turned into a stately palm tree or a zizyphus tree with spreading branches, I thought to myself as I walked on between the graves. I was walking slowly, guided by the faint light of that lamp. I walked a long way before I reached the main road. I put out my arm in the hope that someone would stop and save me from my predicament. The mosques started reciting the Qur'an and dawn was approaching. Finally, a taxi stopped and the driver offered to help me. I told him I was a stranger without any money, I wanted to go to Baghdad and when I arrived I would give him whatever he wanted. The compassionate driver agreed and gave me a ride.

60

I'm now in Baghdad, Father, staying in a hotel as strangers do. I'm looking at your picture propped up on the bedside table, not hanging from a black ribbon, and I'm lighting a candle for you. You don't need one of these black sashes across the corner of the frame because anyone who saw bones lined up under a skull would never imagine they belonged to someone who was still breathing. The Baghdad air you knew is no longer clean, Father. The identity card war has poisoned it. Sectarian bastards are dancing on the remains of the city and rubbing salt into its wounds. Did I tell you that the pictures of the man who had you buried alive have now been torn down? Or that a large statue of him was toppled and the head was dragged along the street with children riding on it? But pictures of other people went up to take the place of the old ones, and a thousand statues have honoured new leaders. Now, Father, we have as many pictures and statues as there are sheep in Australia. And the strange thing is that every one of these sheep wears some symbol of holiness on its chest. Would you believe it? The country seems to have turned into an incubator for sacred sheep. It's as if someone put a sign on the door saying "Incubator for sanctities". As for the palaces of the tyrant (may he be beaten as soundly as a drum on feast day) and his party buildings and the dens of his followers, they've been turned into palaces for minor tyrants, and dens and party offices for the novices who follow them. We now have as many party offices as there are sushi restaurants in the whole of Japan. Maybe this is because of our unique, distinctive character, since in other countries where tyrants have fallen, their palaces and party offices have been turned into museums where people can learn from the past, or into orphanages, or at the very least into grain silos. But we have turned the party offices into party offices, by God, the patron of success! Didn't I tell you we are a unique, unusual people?

Father, the darkness that you and your comrades tried to disperse, by lighting a candle, still covers the country and surrounds it on all sides. That darkness still reigns, the bastards are still playing us for fools and sucking our blood like mosquitoes, under new slogans no less absurd than the previous ones. I don't want to pester you, since you have enough troubles of your own, but I'd like to tell you that, frankly speaking, you failed twice – once in your life and once in your death, because your life was no life and your death was no death. And I – sorry, Father – don't want to be a failure like you, so I've decided to leave.

"You're going to run away again, you coward?"

"Yes, I'm going to run away. I can't bear to see all this destruction."

"So why did you get off your arse and come here, then?"

"I came for your sake, and I thought the country was back on its feet and Baghdad was paradise. That's what people tricked me into believing, but what I've seen has shattered my illusions."

"If you'd loved Baghdad, you'd have stayed and struggled for its sake."

"Oh, Father! Struggle? That word is quite the blast from the past! And how did you end up after this struggle? As a pile of bones in a mass grave. Would you like me to end up in a mass grave, just so you won't call me a coward? Oh no, Father, I'd rather stay above ground and you can call me a coward as much as you like."

"But the days of mass graves are over and will never return."

"Who says? If you'd been with me on this trip through the countryside, you'd have a different opinion. And if you'd seen what I've seen, and heard what I've heard, you'd tell me to get the hell out of here."

"So, is there no hope, my son?"

"Hope, you say? There is hope, Father, but it's been kidnapped, tied up with thick ropes and thrown into a dark cell, and the door's been locked."

"And where's the key?"

"The key's hidden in the fifty-sixth fold in the turban of a heretic sheikh who loves money and power."

I was frightened I might end up as a pile of bones in a black bag, scattered on the roadway, my head crushed by a speeding truck. I was worried the tragedy might be repeated, that Baghdad would deny me, like you, a grave where I could rest in peace, so I've decided to leave again. But this time I will leave in search of a decent death, not a decent life. There, in the land of the favoured, I will seek a gentle death, not a death at the hands of young men armed to the teeth with holy ignorance and destructive beliefs. I'll look for a grave like the grave of my neighbour Jakob Jondal, so that I can rest in peace and tranquillity. I'll go back to Norway and be laid to rest in the cherry orchard. As for you, Father, the most I can do is tell them to bury your picture with me, and maybe your soul will enjoy peace and quiet.

61

The next morning, I went to the hospital, had the plaster cast on my chest changed and asked them about the stitches in my forehead. They said they hadn't dried out yet and it would take more time for them to heal. That meant I would go back to Norway with the mark of a painful memory on my forehead, I said to myself before leaving the hospital. I went to the shops and bought a new charger for my phone and a top-up card: I hadn't used the phone since I came out of that dungeon. Then I went back to the hotel and waited till nightfall, when Abir would be on her own and could take my call. I dialled her number and she answered straight away, as if her finger had been resting on the button. She said she had tried to call me a thousand times but my phone had been out of service. I told her what had happened to me there and she cried. She blamed herself, since she had been the reason I had come back to Baghdad. She said they hadn't been able to get to the mass grave that day because a rogue checkpoint near Latifiya had stopped them, arrested two of her colleagues and then executed them on the roadway in front of her eyes. She'd had a breakdown and fallen ill watching her colleagues pleading for their lives, so she had been off work for the days following the incident.

I didn't tell her I had decided to go back to Norway but I asked her not to blame herself too much and suggested we meet to have a chat. I wanted to see her at least once before I left.

"Abir, how about we meet tomorrow?" I said.

"I'd like that. When and where?"

"Eight in the evening, in Karrada. How would that suit you?"

"Suits me fine."

"Okay, agreed. Sleep well."

"You too."

62

Suhail, the nice hotel worker, left the room and shut the door behind him after filling the fridge with bottles of beer and mineral water. I lay on the bed and tried to sleep, but suddenly I had an excruciating headache. The pain was like a giant wrestler who had decided to finish off his opponent in the first round. In its grip I was twisting and turning like a cowardly mouse. I fended it off with a tranquillizer and turned on my laptop. The headache accepted a truce and gradually started to fade away. I opened my email account in case someone had sent me an important message. All I found was a few routine messages. I clicked on the pictures folder and started to browse through the pictures of Abir one by one. The headache seemed to have disappeared completely. I put the laptop aside, put out the light and shut my eyes, my hands folded over my chest, reminiscing about my long-distance flirtation with Abir, which began with a short message and expanded until the words would have filled a whole book full of passion and impatient desire. I wonder why people are inclined to undervalue and make fun of this kind of love. What does love have to do with distance?

If I hadn't gone through that experience after my visit to the mass grave, I would have said I was as lucky as a pampered poodle. I say this with complete confidence because I had a girlfriend and her pictures eased my pain. But I had decided to go, and that was the end of it. I would go back alone and we would be destined to meet only this once, because Abir was like a fish: she would die if she left Baghdad. In case she wouldn't recognise me, I told her that at our meeting I would be wearing jeans and a white shirt. She didn't need to wear or carry anything distinctive, because I remembered exactly what she looked like: pretty with honey-coloured eyes, short brown hair, medium height, as slim as an orchid and as meek as a dove.

63

I arrived early. Karrada was lit up and crowded, unlike other parts of Baghdad. The streets were full of people and the pavements cluttered with stalls and pedlars' carts. All the city needed was more security. I passed the time looking at the knick-knacks, little statues and paintings on sale in the galleries in the Asfar market. A large picture hanging on the façade of one gallery caught my attention and I stopped to look at it for some time. Done in oil paint on canvas, it showed a dignified man sitting in a café reading the newspaper with steam rising from the cup of tea in front of him. For some reason I felt I recognised the man. Maybe because I wished my father were still alive and hadn't been buried. I left the art market and walked to the main street, stopping a while at a stall selling keyrings and leather belts, with a friendly young man sitting behind it. I asked if he could shorten my belt for me, since I had lost seven pounds weight and my jeans were now rather too big for me. "Sure," he said. In case I lost more weight he punched two new holes in the belt, rather than just one. I thanked him and walked on. I headed north till I ended up outside a shop that sold fruit juices, with an illuminated sign saying,

"Jabbar the Sherbet Man". I felt thirsty when I saw a small fountain of juice gushing up from among the piles of fruit carefully arranged in the shop window. It was a neat shop window with oranges, pomegranates and bananas hanging down on wires, and the lights added a certain cheerfulness. Mains electricity appears on the wish list of most Iraqis. Suhail says the government doesn't want to repair the electricity network in order to make it easier for people to go to heaven. When I asked him what electricity had to do with heaven, he said in his spontaneous sarcastic way, "Praying a lot gets you to heaven, and whenever the electricity comes back on we all shout, 'O God, bless the Prophet Muhammad and his family.' So they turn it on and off often."

I ordered a glass of pomegranate juice and stepped aside while he made it. I suddenly had a pain in my stomach, like the pains that orphans have after a long hungry night. I clutched my stomach and the pain moved to my chest and then disappeared, leaving a heavy sensation that's difficult to explain. But I soon forgot about it and watched the passers-by instead. I love streets crowded with pedestrians. Every person's face tells a different story, except for Iraqis, whose stories are predictably sad. Be Iraqi, be sad! I'll go home with memories of thousands of sad faces and from the top of Mount Galdhøpiggen, Norway's highest mountain, I'll complain to the heavens on their behalf.

My mobile phone rang. it was Abir.

"Hi, Said," she said.

"Hi, Abir, where have you got to?"

"I've just got out of the taxi."

She was unusually flustered and I could hear she was out of breath.

"Where are you?" she asked.

"I'm here, at Jabbar the Sherbet Guy's shop."

"Ah, that means I'm close by."

"Good. I'll order a fruit juice for you. Abir . . . hello?"

The line cut off before I could ask what she would like to drink. Maybe she couldn't hear me because of the noise so she called off, or maybe her phone battery died on her and the phone cut out. Anyway, I didn't try to call her back. I would order her a pomegranate juice anyway, because the pomegranate juice in Karrada is unbeatable.

I went up to the man at the counter and asked him to make it two pomegranate juices with extra ice, and then waited for Abir. Finally, she turned up. I recognised her even before she waved to me from a distance. She was wearing a grey skirt and a long-sleeved white blouse. "There you are, sir," said the juice man, handing me two large glasses of freshly made pomegranate juice. Although I was very thirsty and the droplets of condensed water on the outside of the glass made it look very tempting, I decided not to drink till Abir arrived and we could share the pleasure. She made "drink it" signs to me in the distance, but I didn't. I just held the glasses and looked at her. At the same moment a gust of wind blew Abir's skirt up in the air, revealing her thighs.

Embarrassed, she pushed it down with a small handbag and picked up pace. She hurried because she knew I was thirsty and couldn't resist the pomegranate juice. She was getting much closer. There were just a few steps between us when a terrible noise rang in my ears, deafened me and knocked the glass out of my hands. For some fractions of a second, I couldn't see or hear anything, and when I came back to my senses I saw that the juice shop now looked like a black hole in the side of the building. Bodies were strewn everywhere, and a mixture of blood and fruit juice traced maps of coloured death on the pavement. What happened in those fractions of a second was a nightmare I could never forget. There were charred and smouldering bodies, mangled limbs still burning, an arm inexplicably dangling from the top of a building, blood-stained shoes that had been ripped off their owners, and broken glass on the bodies of the victims and on the sides of the road. The sound of ambulances rang throughout Karrada and people rushed to the horrible scene to look for their loved ones. I saw a woman barefoot in a dress but with no abaya, running towards us, beating her head and cheeks and shouting, "Muhannad, Muhannad, Muhannad." I heard someone say that her son Muhannad had been selling leather belts on the pavement outside the juice shop. The fire had no doubt consumed him, along with the belts. I looked for Abir but I couldn't find her among the dead bodies. I wandered through the rubble in search of her. In the end

I found her lying close to a small ditch that ran along the pavement. She was a charred corpse.

Among the people in the street at the time I seemed to be the only survivor. Some bastard had stuffed tonnes of explosives into a car parked outside the juice shop, and at the press of a button it exploded, scoring yet another famous victory over juices. I really don't know how I managed to emerge safe and sound. I felt my face, my body, my arms and legs: everything was in place. I tried to help the firemen put out the fire but they did their work and left without needing me. The police also left after dispersing the onlookers and drawing a routine sketch of the incident. All the ambulances left too, except for one that was carrying two bodies and looking to see if there were any more, or any limbs hanging in the juice shop. As I watched them, I felt a burning pain in my chest. The incident left a deep and incurable wound in the heart of Baghdad, adding to the city's anguish, gloom and sorrow.

Looking around I saw the body of a man who'd been thrown to the other side of the street by the force of the blast. There wasn't enough light to tell if he was dead or not. I hurried over and found it was a lifeless corpse lying face down on the pavement, his clothes torn. I called after the ambulance men to come back and pick up the body but they were too far off. I turned the body face up. He was a thin, middle-aged man, his jeans and white shirt shredded by the explosion. I looked into his face, which seemed familiar despite the burns and saw two stitches at the top of his forehead. I turned around and saw my father standing looking at me with unusual tenderness. His face was completely uncovered, handsome and radiant despite the deep wrinkles that sadness had etched into his forehead. I put out my hand to him and he finally took it, and we vanished together.

Postscript

At 8.25 a.m. on Friday, the accidents and emergencies department at Oslo General Hospital received a phone call from Barbara, the cleaner in the Venus building, which lies in the middle of the Hellerud district in the east of the city. The caller said she had found Mr Said Jensen lying on the floor in his flat on the ninth floor of the building, inside the study, and that he was having convulsions and was unconscious. The paramedics arrived at 8.34 a.m. but it was too late for first aid. Mr Jensen's heart had stopped and he was dead. The next day the post-mortem report said that the cause of death was an overdose of ketamine.

The manuscript of a novel was found on the desk and Mr Jensen appears to have finished writing it some hours before his death. There was also a letter addressed to Helena Jorstad, editor-in-chief at *Dagposten* newspaper. The manuscript and the letter were delivered to Ms Jorstad, who proceeded to open the envelope sadly and in puzzlement. There was a short request on the part of Said Jensen – that his story and the hallucinations about his trip to Baghdad should be published, and that he should be given a gravestone so that he should not be forgotten, which would be like a second death.

Helena spent that night crying, with her friend's novel in her hands. He had passed away too soon, without saying goodbye. In the morning, after reading it, she contacted the heirs of Mr Jakob Jondal, the neighbour who had died several years earlier, and obtained their written permission to bury Said there. Said's body spent a few days in the morgue and Helena then arranged a burial under the shade of the cherry trees in a ceremony attended by his colleagues at the *Dagposten* and a group of his readers and admirers. Finally, she buried with him the frame that had been hanging in the study, and she had the gravestone inscribed with the words:

> *Here lies Said Jensen*
> *Glory to those at Rest in the Cherry Orchard*

The translator
Oslo, 2010

About the Author

Azher Jirjees is an Iraqi writer and novelist, born in Baghdad in 1973. From 2003, he worked as a journalist in Iraq and published a number of articles and stories in local and Arab newspapers and periodicals. In 2005, he wrote a satirical book about terrorist militias entitled *The Earthly Hell*, which resulted in an assassination attempt against him and he was forced to flee the country. He fled to Syria, then Morocco and finally to Norway, where he now lives permanently. His other works include two short story collections, *Fouq Bilad al-Sawad* (Above the Country of Blackness, 2015) and *Saani' al-Halwa* (The Sweetmaker, 2017), and two novels. His first novel is *At Rest in the Cherry Orchard* (*al-Nawm fi Haql al-Karaz*, 2019), and was longlisted for the 2020 International Prize for Arabic Fiction. His second novel *Hajar al-Sa'ada* (Stone of Happiness) was shortlisted for the same prize in 2023. He works as a freelance translator between Arabic and Norwegian.

About the Translator

Jonathan Wright is an award-winning translator of contemporary fiction by Arab authors. His translations include works by Basma Abdel Aziz, Ahmed Taibaoui, Mazen Maarouf, Amjad Nasser, Ahmed Saadawi, Hassan Blasim, Saud Alsanousi, Sinan Antoon, Youssef Ziedan, Hamour Ziada, Ezzedine C. Fishere, Khaled el-Khamissi, Bahaa Abdelmegid, Rasha al-Ameer, and others. He studied Arabic, Turkish and Islamic History at St. John's College, University of Oxford, and worked for many years as a journalist in the Arab world including in Tunisia, Oman, Lebanon and Egypt.

OTHER TITLES FROM BANIPAL BOOKS

The Secrets of Folder 42 by Abdelmajid Sebbata. ISBN: 978-1-913043-41-4 • Pbk & Ebook • 368pp • 2024. Translated from the Arabic by Raphael Cohen. In this thriller-cum-jigsaw puzzle, two storylines play out across continents and true historical events as American novelist Christine McMillan and student Rachid Bennacer aim to solve The Secrets of Folder 42, while chess champion Zouhair Belkacem, shunted off to medical school in Moscow, returns to Morocco in time for a spectacular crunch day.

Birds of Nabaa, A Mauritanian Tale by Abdallah Uld Mohamadi Bah. ISBN: 978-1-913043-43-8 • Pbk & Ebook • 192pp • 2023. Translated from the Arabic by Raphael Cohen. This first Mauritanian novel in English translation from Arabic is a tale of physical and spiritual journeys, introducing diverse characters, poetry, Sufi dancing and the world's first climate-change refugee.

Shadow of the Sun by Taleb Alrefai. ISBN: 978-1-913043-36-0 • Pbk & Ebook • 192pp • 2023. Translated from the Arabic by Nashwa Nasreldin. Impoverished Egyptian teacher Helmy is desperate to find a better life for himself, his wife and little boy, seeing no future in Cairo. He dreams of working in oil-rich Kuwait.

The Stone Serpent, Barates of Palmyra's Elegy for Regina his Beloved – An Eastern Serenade by Nouri al-Jarrah. Translated from the Arabic by Catherine Cobham. ISBN: 978-1-913043-29-2 • 2022 • 112pp • Pbk & Ebook. Syrian poet al-Jarrah restores to life an ancient story of migrant Syrian life, love and freedom, after a single line in Aramaic on a tombstone at Arabeia Roman Fort, Hadrian's Wall, sparks his imagination.

Things I Left Behind by Shada Mustafa. Translated from the Arabic by Nancy Roberts. ISBN: 978-1-913043-26-1 • 2022 • 128pp • Pbk & Ebook. This debut novel by a young Palestinian woman interrogates the memories of growing up to find liberation from the continual pain and tragic anguish of the "things" she left behind in her childhood in an occupied and divided land and family.

The Tent Generations, Palestinian Poems. Selected, introduced, and translated by Mohammed Sawaie. ISBN: 978-1-913043-18-6 • 2022 • 160pp • Pbk & Ebook. The 16 twentieth-century Palestinian poets are witness for today's readers of displacement, disapora and occupation, through 1948, 1967 and 1973, war after war.

Sarajevo Firewood by Saïd Khatibi. Translated from the Arabic by Paul Starkey. ISBN 978-1-913043-23-0 • 2021 • 320pp • Pbk & Ebook. A searing novel exploring the legacy of the recent histories and civil wars in both Algeria and Bosnia-Herzegovina and the traumatic experience of exile for so many.

Fadhil Al-Azzawi's Beautiful Creatures by Iraqi author Fadhil al-Azzawi. ISBN 978-1-913043-10-0 • 2021 • 152pp • Hbk, Pbk, Ebook. An open poetic work, written in defiance of the "sanctity of genre", translated from the Arabic by the author, and edited by Hannah Somerville.

The Madness of Despair by Ghalya F T Al Said. Translated from the Arabic by Raphael Cohen. ISBN: 978-1-913043-12-4 • 2021 • 256pp • Hbk, Pbk, Ebook. The first of the Omani author's six novels in English translation is a powerful saga of how psychological suffering and cultural displacement upsets very ordinary aspirations for life and love.

Poems of Alexandria and New York by Ahmed Morsi. Translated from the Arabic by Raphael Cohen. ISBN 978-1-913043-16-2 • 2021 • 126pp • Pbk & Ebook. First volume in English translation for renowned Egyptian painter, art critic, and poet.

Mansi: A Rare Man in His Own Way by Tayeb Salih. Translated and introduced by Adil Babikir. ISBN 978-0-9956369-8-9 • Pbk & Ebook • 184pp • 2020. This affectionate memoir of Salih's irrepressible friend Mansi shows a new side to the Sudanese author, renowned for his classic novel *Season of Migration to the North*.

Goat Mountain by Habib Selmi.Translated from the Arabic by Charis Olszok. ISBN: 978-1-913043-04-9 • 2020 • Pbk & Ebook • 92pp. The well-known Tunisian author's acclaimed debut novel, from 1988, now in English translation.

The Mariner by Taleb Alrefai. Translated from the Arabic by Russell Harris. ISBN: 978-1-913043-08-7 • Pbk & Ebook • 160pp • 2020. A fictional re-telling of the final sea journey of famous Kuwaiti dhow shipmaster Captain Al-Najdi.

A Boat to Lesbos, and other poems by Nouri Al-Jarrah. Translated from the Arabic by Camilo Gómez-Rivas and Allison Blecker, with paintings by Reem Yassouf. ISBN: 978-0-9956369-4-1 • 2018 • Pbk • 120pp. The first book in English translation for this major Syrian poet bears passionate witness – through the eye of history, Sappho and Odysseus – to Syrian families fleeing to Lesbos.

An Iraqi In Paris by Samuel Shimon. ISBN: 978-0-9574424-8-1 • Pbk • 282pp • 2016. Translated from the Arabic by Christina Philips and Piers Amodia with the author. "A gem of autobiographical writing", "a manifesto of tolerance".

Heavenly Life: Selected Poems by Ramsey Nasr. ISBN: 978-0-9549666-9-0 • 2010 • Pbk • 180pp. First English-language collection for Ramsey Nasr, Poet Laureate of the Netherlands 2009 & 2010. Translated from the Dutch by David Colmer. Introduced by Victor Schiferli with Foreword by Ruth Padel.

Knife Sharpener: Selected Poems by Sargon Boulus. The first English-language collection for the renowned late Iraqi poet. ISBN: 978-0-9549666-7-6 • 2009 • Pbk • 154pp. Foreword by Adonis. Poems translated from the Arabic by the author. Plus tributes by fellow authors and Afterword by the publisher.

Shepherd of Solitude: Selected Poems by Amjad Nasser. Translated from the Arabic and introduced by Khaled Mattawa. ISBN: 978-0-9549666-8-3 • 2009 • Pbk • 186pp. First English-language collection for the late major Jordanian poet.

Mordechai's Moustache and his Wife's Cats, and other stories by Mahmoud Shukair. ISBN: 978-0-9549666-3-8 • 2007 • Pbk • 124pp. Translated from the Arabic by Issa J Boullata, Elizabeth Whitehouse, Elizabeth Winslow and Christina Phillips. First major English publication of Palestine's maestro storyteller.

A Retired Gentleman, & other stories by Issa J Boullata. ISBN: 978-0-9549666-6-9 • 2007 • Pbk • 120pp. Emigrant tales from the Jerusalem-born author and scholar.

The Myrtle Tree by Lebanese Jad El Hage. ISBN: 978-0-9549666-4-5 • 2007 • Pbk • 288pp. "This remarkable novel, set in a Lebanese mountain village, conveys with razor-sharp accuracy the sights, sounds, tastes and tragic dilemmas of Lebanon's fratricidal civil war. A must read" – Patrick Seale.

Sardines and Oranges: Short Stories from North Africa. Introduced by Peter Clark. ISBN: 978-0-9549666-1-4 • 2005 • Pbk • 222pp. The 26 stories from Algeria, Egypt, Morocco, Sudan and Tunisia are by 21 authors, all translated from the Arabic bar one, Mohammed Dib's from French.